ALSO BY MICHAEL RIDPATH

Magnus Iceland Mysteries

Where the Shadows Lie

66 Degrees North/Far North (US)

Meltwater

Sea of Stone

The Wanderer

Death in Dalvik

Writing in Ice: A Crime Writer's Guide to Iceland

Thrillers

The Diplomat's Wife

Launch Code

Amnesia

Traitor's Gate

Shadows of War

WHALE FJORD

MICHAEL RIDPATH

YARMER

First published in Great Britain in 2024 by Yarmer Head.

ISBN: 978-1-7396121-0-8

for Will

HVALFJÖRDUR
N
Hvalfjördur
Tóftir
Hvammsvík
Selvík
Laxahóll
Akranes
Esja
Kollafjördur
Mosfellsbaer
Reykjavík
Hafnarfjördur
Keflavík
0
50 km

ONE

September 2023

Gerdur's Hollow had terrified Jón when he was a little boy.

Even now, after spending the entire fifty-eight years of his life on the farm of Selvík on whose margins it lay, it made him uneasy.

It was his grandmother's fault. She had told him about Gerdur, the witch who had lived in a hovel along the track between Selvík and the larger, more prosperous, neighbouring farm at Laxahóll. Sometime in the distant past, Gerdur had lain a curse upon the farmer at Laxahóll, and his daughter had died. Appalled, the locals had turned on her and stoned her to death, burying her in a shallow cave covered with rocks in the hollow, which from then on bore her name.

The hollow lay in a fold in the steep, rock-strewn hillside, out of sight of the road. It was a dangerous place. This was either because it was haunted by the tormented Gerdur, or because the rock face was unstable, or both.

According to Jón's grandmother, there used to be a small cairn at the base of the hollow. Anyone who ventured in there was supposed to place a stone on the cairn. Once, eighty years ago, Jón's grandfather had omitted to do this, and the following night there had been an earthquake which loosened the stones and toppled the cairn.

Since then, Jón's grandfather, then his father and then Jón himself had avoided the spot if they possibly could. If a sheep got lost in there, Jón would send in his sheepdog to fetch it out.

Jón swung his mallet down on to the fence post. It was early September, and white clouds rolled into and then out of the valley, impelled by a stiff cool breeze hurrying from the sea fifteen kilometres to the west. Soon he and his neighbours would be rounding up their sheep on the hills to bring them back down to their farms. The fences had to be ready. Jón should have had his own son to help him with this work, but the boy had been taken away from the farm by his mother when he was only eight, and now he was studying for his accountancy exams in Reykjavík. Big strong lad too. A waste.

The boundary between Selvík and its larger neighbour lay in a bend in the valley of the Selá, a clear, fast-moving river rippling with salmon and sea trout that hurried down past the farm to Hvalfjördur – the Whale Fjord – sparkling in the sunshine a kilometre away. The valley narrowed at this point, allowing only a few acres of meagre meadow for Selvík. Further upstream, broad, lush green fields fed the horses, sheep and cattle of the wealthy Laxahóll farmers. Thus had it always been.

Jón stood up straight, and was preparing a mightier swing, when he heard a cry.

He looked up.

Two figures were running towards him from the direction of Gerdur's Hollow, shouting and waving. A man and a woman dressed in bright rain jackets. Hikers.

They had got themselves into some kind of trouble. Idiots. Perhaps a friend had tried to climb up the scree and fallen.

'Hey! Hey!' The man in front was shouting and waving at him.

Jón waited.

The man stumbled over the tussocks of yellow grass until he was panting in front of Jón. He was in his thirties, short and dumpy, and unfit by the look of him. His trailing girlfriend was shorter and dumpier and even more unfit.

'We found something!' the hiker said, in English.

'What?' Jón asked, curtly, also in English. Foreigners. Not surprising they had got themselves into trouble.

The man swallowed. He seemed distressed. Scared even. Despite himself, Jón felt that fear transfer on to him.

'What?' Jón repeated.

'A skull.'

Jón blinked, and then pulled himself together. 'An animal skull? A sheep?'

'No. A human skull.'

'Are you sure?'

'Quite sure.'

The hiker's companion staggered up next to him. 'It's definitely a human skull,' she said.

'Show me.'

Jón was a tall man with long strides and he was used to walking over rough ground. Kappi, his black-and-white sheepdog, bounded along beside him. The hikers had to run to keep up. A pair of ravens circled, watchful, overhead.

He remembered as if it were yesterday his grandmother

warning him about the hollow. As he had grown up and become a father himself, he understood how the story had probably developed over the years as a means of keeping children away from what was a genuinely dangerous area of steep, unstable rocks and scree. Yet he had also learned that historical documents showed a witch had indeed been arrested and executed in these parts in the seventeenth century.

He was determined not to let his nervousness show.

A short, steep bank of yellow grass led up to a twist in the hillside and a dark gully shaded from the sun. Jón sent Kappi in first, just to be on the safe side.

The hillside rose up above him about a hundred metres. The hollow itself was a scar only a few metres wide, which had been filled with stones and rocks the last time Jón had seen it the previous summer. Things had shifted since then. Rocks had fallen. Somewhere beneath the debris, water trickled. The air was dead here, out of the wind.

For the last couple of years, there had been a swarm of earthquakes throughout the south-west of Iceland accompanying the volcanic eruptions on the Reykjanes peninsula eighty kilometres away. They were rarer and less severe in the Hvalfjördur region. Not enough to bring down mountainsides, but occasionally enough to shift loose stone.

'Where?' Jón snapped.

The male hiker led him to a boulder a couple of metres up from the bottom.

'Bettina was sitting on that. I was taking her picture. And then she saw it.'

Jón glanced at the girl. 'Behind the rock,' she said, pointing.

Jón climbed up on to the boulder and looked down the other side.

Sure enough, two blank eye sockets stared back up at him out of a cracked sphere of bone.

Struggling to hide his fear from the two hikers, he reached for his phone.

TWO

10 May 1940

0530. *Units of the German 1st Panzer division under General Heinz Guderian cross the Luxembourg border at Wallendorf, leading a column of tanks and infantry-filled trucks stretching back a hundred kilometres. The German invasion of Luxembourg, Belgium, Holland and France begins.*

0620. *746 men of the British Royal Marines steam into Reykjavík harbour aboard four warships. They land at the docks. An Icelandic policeman asks the crowd on the quay-side to make way for them. The British invasion of Iceland has begun.*

Captain Neville Pybus-Smith knocked back his fourth whisky and ordered another. The tall blond barman refilled his glass with a hint of a smile. He had seemed stiff and unfriendly when Neville had entered the Hotel Borg with the British Consul and a couple of marine officers two hours before for a swift one. Perhaps the natives were warming up to their new guests? Good to see.

The diplomat and the marine captain had left after just one drink, but a lieutenant of about Neville's own age named Cranshaw had been happy to stay and keep him company. Like Neville, Cranshaw was not a regular officer, but had joined up at the outbreak of war. Neville had worked at a merchant bank in the City; Cranshaw had sold cars in Bedford. Neville had had longer strings to pull than the likes of Cranshaw and so had managed to join military intelligence with the rank of captain – quite a coup. It was partly down to his fluent German, but mostly to the people he knew.

Like all salesmen, Lieutenant Cranshaw was good company over a drink.

'Can I get you another, old man?' Neville asked him.

Cranshaw checked his watch. 'No, I'd better turn in. Up early tomorrow. Plenty to do.'

'Right-oh.' Neville nodded. There certainly was a lot to do. But for now, he wanted to savour their victory. 'See you in the morning.'

It had been a long, busy, successful day. Being an army intelligence officer, not a marine like the rest of the invading force, Neville had been among the first ashore. The top-hatted British Consul General had been waiting for him as arranged, and, with the escort of a platoon of marines, they had marched up the road from the harbour to the German consulate. It was a small grey house in a little garden set back from the road. A red metal plate with a black swastika was fixed to the wall by the front door.

Neville was alarmed to see smoke spilling out of an upstairs window.

He rapped at the door with the butt of his revolver. It was answered eventually by the German Consul General himself in his dressing gown, trembling with rage. The man was imposing: very tall – at least six feet six – blond, his face scored with duelling scars.

'What do you want?' he demanded.

'We wish to come in,' the British diplomat replied politely in German.

'For what purpose?'

'To take over your Consulate General.'

'But this is a neutral country!'

'So was Denmark, Herr Consul General.'

Neville pushed past the German into the house and ran up the stairs. He found a bath reeking of petrol, full of burning documents. He turned on the taps to douse the flames and was able to save some of the papers, which were now safely back on HMS *Glasgow* in the harbour.

While the British diplomats moved on to meet the Icelandic Prime Minister, Neville began the task of mopping up the Germans in Reykjavík. British intelligence had suggested that there were quite a number of them, and they had been preparing to overthrow the Icelandic government themselves.

That was why Churchill had ordered the pre-emptive invasion of Iceland. He had learned from the last war how important the North Atlantic was to the survival of Britain; if the Germans gained control of the island of Iceland, they would secure a lethal base for their aircraft and submarines to attack British shipping. Iceland was neutral, but then so had Norway and Denmark been, and yet the Germans had invaded them in April, overrunning both countries before the British could properly come to their aid.

Churchill wasn't going to be caught out like that again.

The British diplomats' visit to the Icelandic Prime Minister had gone as well as could be expected. Although still a possession of the Danish Crown, Iceland had gained independence over its own domestic affairs. Howard Smith, the new British Minister for Iceland who had arrived with the marines, had explained that Britain had invaded the country to protect her from the Germans, and that the British had no intention of interfering with her government.

Hermann Jónasson, the Prime Minister, replied that he didn't believe that the Germans would have invaded, but since the British had arrived with good intentions his country would cooperate. It would have been nice to have been asked first. He then made a radio broadcast to his countrymen asking them to consider the British soldiers their guests and to show them all courtesy.

It was unclear how many Germans there were in Reykjavík. Sixty-two had been recently rescued from a sunk German freighter and were now staying in two hotels in the capital. Neville had managed to round up fifty-three of these and send them back to HMS *Glasgow*. There were no doubt more to find, as well as possible wireless transmitters. Intelligence suggested there were pro-Nazi Icelanders to be dealt with, including, most worryingly, the chief of police.

There was still plenty to do. But for now, Neville would enjoy his whisky.

The Borg was the best hotel in Reykjavík – the only decent hotel in Reykjavík. As the intelligence officer, Neville knew this and had been quick to snag a room.

It was getting late and the bar was thinning out. Curious locals had gathered there to observe the British officers who had dropped in for a drink. Some had spoken to the invaders, mostly telling them they were happy that it was the British and not the other lot who had invaded.

Most of the drinkers were men, but there were a number of women in the bar as well. Neville was already quite taken with the women in Iceland. It wasn't just that an uncommonly large number of them were blonde and beautiful. It was the way they held themselves – erect, proud, strong – that gave him a frisson of, well, desire.

He had his eye on a table of three Icelanders who had come in soon after him: a lean, spare man in a double-breasted suit, and two women, one blonde and one red-haired. He had noticed the women glancing at him a couple of times, once exchanging a laugh and a smile between themselves. He knew he looked good in his khaki uniform. He was thirty: dark hair, dark eyes and a thin dark moustache which offset his prominent front teeth, or so he hoped. He didn't exactly resemble Clark Gable, but he looked more like him than the fair-haired oafs of Iceland.

Now, on his fifth whisky, at the end of a day of high excitement, Neville's thoughts turned to sex.

He had been married for six years to a woman whose good looks had fattened out within a year of their wedding. Peggy didn't like sex. She put up with it, and their matrimonial duty had produced two very sweet but often annoying daughters. To be honest, Neville didn't like sex with Peggy much either.

But he did like the idea of sex. Especially with that redhead.

They were leaving. As the redhead passed him on the way to the exit, she looked straight at him. It was a frank, slightly haughty stare.

It was electrifying.

Neville was pretty sure that the man was with the blonde woman. Unless they all lived together, at some point they would split up.

Neville wanted to see where that point was.

He downed his whisky and followed them out of the hotel into the grassy square in front of the Parliament building.

The three figures walked towards the harbour together. They paused in front of the impressive Eimskip shipping company head office, emblazoned with a jarring swastika-like emblem, to wish each other goodnight. Then the couple turned left and the redhead turned right.

Neville wasn't sure how to approach her, so he followed her discreetly while he came up with a plan. Would she speak English?

Perhaps that wouldn't matter.

He found the prospect of making love to a woman with whom he couldn't communicate at all even more exciting.

It was ten o'clock and not yet dark, although the light was fading to gloom under low clouds, leaving a late-evening chill in the air. Reykjavík was a town of corrugated metal – the shops and houses were clad with metal roofs and metal walls on concrete foundations – but Neville was cheered to see lights twinkling inside them, unlike the severe, treacherous blackouts in English cities.

The woman crossed a main road and climbed a hill, entering a narrow street bordered on either side by more brightly painted metal houses. A small squad of marines marched past, bayonets fixed. She stared at them. They stared at her.

She turned into an even narrower lane. Neville realized that she might be close to her destination. It was now or never.

He quickened his pace, almost to a run. 'I say, excuse me!' he called.

The woman stopped and turned. A look of puzzlement turned into a frown.

'Do you speak English?'

'*Ég skil ekki.*'

Clearly not. That explained the frown then.

'I saw you in the hotel,' Neville said with his most charming grin, made a little more charming by the alcohol.

'*Ég skil ekki,*' the woman repeated. Neville had no idea what that meant.

'The Hotel Borg?' No sign of understanding from the woman. She must have known what he meant by 'the Hotel Borg'.

He pointed to his chest. 'Neville,' he said. Then pointed to her. 'Your name?'

The woman hunched her shoulders and turned away, muttering something to herself.

Neville touched her arm. She shook him off. He grabbed her arm harder.

He wanted this woman. The fact they didn't speak each other's language didn't matter. He would make her understand how beautiful he thought she was, how much he wanted her.

He pulled her around.

She turned and stared at him, her eyes blazing. She said something and tried to break away.

He tightened his grip. 'You know you are the most gorgeous woman in Iceland,' he said, realizing as he did so that he had slurred the word 'Iceland' to 'Isheland'.

She slapped him.

He dropped his hand and stared at her. 'I say, you can't do that. I'm a British officer!'

'Sir?'

Neville turned to see a sergeant moving sharply towards him.

He could feel himself reddening. He took a step back from the woman. 'Sergeant.'

'Is this woman bothering you, sir?'

The sergeant was a few years younger than Neville, and many ranks lower. But he had that infernal air of authority that regular NCOs in the British Army, or the marines for that matter, managed to convey. He knew Neville wasn't a proper soldier.

And at that moment his blue eyes were cold with contempt.

Neville drew himself up to his full height. He was an officer, dammit.

'Would you like me to arrest her, sir?' the sergeant asked.

Would he? Of course not. Neville felt himself drowning in shame. 'No. No. That's quite all right, sergeant.' He tried and failed to assert some authority. 'Carry on,' he said inconsequentially.

The sergeant ignored him. 'Run along now, miss,' he said to the woman, his tone firm but kind.

With a final glare at Neville, she hurried up the hill.

'You never can be too careful with the locals,' said the sergeant. And with a smart salute that somehow dripped with irony, he returned to his squad of soldiers who had been watching.

Crushed, humiliated, Neville returned to the Hotel Borg and bed.

THREE

September 2023

'Come on, Magnús, get a move on! This is a suspicious death we are investigating.'

Magnus bit into his *kleina* – a kind of Icelandic doughnut – and stayed resolutely within the speed limit. His colleague, Vigdís, had been impatient when he had stopped for the pastry and a coffee. He navigated the mini-roundabouts around Mosfellsbaer carefully and settled in behind a squat truck laden with construction rubble travelling at fifty kilometres an hour.

'Now you're just winding me up,' said Vigdís.

'It's a skeleton, Vigdís. It will wait. God knows how many years it's waited so far.'

'Well, neither will we until we get there.'

Normally, Magnus appreciated Icelanders' impatience to go places fast and get things done, but sometimes it could be exhausting. He was an Icelander himself, of course, but he had been brought up in America and spent the first ten years of his police career in Boston.

'You're just worried Edda will get there before us, aren't you?'

Edda was head of the Forensics Unit. Meticulous and thorough once she was doing her job, she and her team prided themselves on how quickly they could get their van to a crime scene. They loved it when they beat CID.

'Maybe.' Vigdís shrugged. 'Suit yourself.' She sipped her own coffee and pulled out her phone. She made a call.

'Hi, Mum. How is she?' Vigdís listened. '*Still* asleep. I suppose that's a good thing. Give me a call when she wakes up.'

'Is Erla ill?' Magnus asked.

'Yes. She's got a bad cold and so I couldn't take her to day care.'

'And you got your mum to look after her?' Magnus was surprised. Vigdís's mother was an alcoholic, sometimes recovering, sometimes not.

'I know.' Vigdís frowned. 'She's been dry since Erla was born. I told her I wouldn't leave her alone with her granddaughter until she'd been dry a year. And it's eighteen months. I think.'

'You think?'

'Well, she says she's been dry, but you never know. Not with Mum.'

'Do you want me to take you back to the station so you can go home?' said Magnus. 'This skull isn't going anywhere.'

Vigdís sighed. 'No, that's OK. I was planning to let her look after Erla soon anyway. And it is over a year . . .' She hesitated.

'What?'

'I was worried she was slurring her words.'

'We can turn around.' Magnus repeated his offer.

Vigdís hesitated. 'No. It'll be fine. She always sounds as if she's slurring her words these days. I think it's the cumulative effect of all that alcohol.'

Magnus and Vigdís had worked together for a long time – over ten years. In some ways, they were both outsiders in the Reykjavík police force. Magnus was the Kani Cop – *Kani* meant Yank. And Vigdís was black. She was actually genetically more American than Magnus – her father had been a serviceman at the American base at Keflavík – although Vigdís had never met him. Her mother was Icelandic, however, and Vigdís was one of the few Icelanders of her age who didn't speak English. In Vigdís's case it was a point of principle: she was fed up with Icelanders assuming she was a foreigner and trying to speak to her in English.

When they reached the Hvalfjördur tunnel, about thirty kilometres north of Reykjavík, where Iceland's national Ring Road plunged dramatically underwater on its way north, Magnus turned right and drove eastwards along the shore of the fjord. It was one of those Icelandic days where the weather was changing every ten minutes, as rainclouds barrelled in from the Atlantic on strong south-westerly winds, and then barrelled off, leaving sunshine and rainbows behind them. The waters of the fjord, ruffled by the wind, changed with the sky, from blue to green to dark grey and back to blue again.

A dusting of early snow had fallen on the mountains on the northern shore. A bright blue aluminium smelter squatted and scowled in a gap between the fells. Iceland's abundant geothermal energy made aluminium-smelting feasible, if controversial.

'God, I hate that plant,' said Magnus. 'It ruins a beautiful fjord.'

'It makes Iceland a twenty-first-century industrial superpower.'

'Yeah, right,' said Magnus. 'Don't tell me you actually like it?'

'OK. I admit it; I don't like it.'

'They could at least paint it a different colour. Maybe camouflage it like they did the warships here during the war.'

'That's actually not a bad idea.'

'You're welcome.'

After several kilometres, they came to a farm and a road signposted to Laxahóll. A small white Toyota was parked on the gravel next to the sign.

'Look!' said Vigdís, pointing out into the water.

Despite its name, there were no whales in Whale Fjord, but Vigdís had spotted half a dozen seals sunning themselves like a string of grey sausages on a group of small seaweed-strewn rocks a few metres from the shore.

'It figures.' Magnus nodded towards the GPS screen in the car. 'That farm's called Selvík.' Seal Bay.

He turned right and drove along a narrow, paved road beside a clear river for a few hundred metres before he came to a little gathering of police cars.

And Edda's forensics van.

'How does she do it?' said Vigdís, shaking her head.

Magnus parked next to the police cars under the scrutiny of half a dozen horses who had trotted over to the corner of their paddock to look, their eyes scarcely visible beneath the thick fringe of their manes. The valley broadened out upstream, lush and peaceful, its green meadows dotted with cylinders of white plastic-coated hay. A large, prosperous set of farm buildings and a small white metal church watched over it.

Magnus began to pull on forensic coveralls, gloves and overshoes.

'Do you really think those are necessary for a skeleton?' Vigdís said.

'If you want to show up to Edda's crime scene without them, that's your choice.'

'Good point.'

Once they were suited up, they walked towards some crime-scene tape in front of a gully scored into the side of the valley.

Magnus didn't recognize the uniformed cop who signed him and Vigdís into the scene – he was from the station in Akranes – but he knew the sergeant, and he knew Edda, of course, who was just getting her equipment ready.

'You guys do take your time,' she said, grinning. She was tall, with long legs, and disconcertingly attractive. She had no difficulty keeping detectives in order. Magnus never messed with her.

'Magnús can't solve a crime without a doughnut,' Vigdís said.

Magnus looked at the gully. It was steep and dark and full of rocks and boulders. At the top, near the ridge, were more rocks.

He scowled. 'That doesn't look very stable.'

'It isn't,' said the sergeant. 'The farmer who found the bodies said there had been a rockfall sometime in the last few months after a small earthquake. That may have been what revealed the bodies.'

'Bodies?' said Magnus. 'I thought there was just one.'

'One skull. Three arms so far. We think we will find a fourth. But we are waiting for forensics to move the rocks.'

'Be careful,' said Magnus to Edda. 'We don't want to lose anyone to another rockfall.'

'Don't worry about us, Magnús,' Edda said, clearly insulted that Magnus should think she would be anything but careful.

'Have you seen the skull yet?'

'Just a quick look. Follow me.'

She led Magnus and Vigdís to a boulder. The skull stared up at them, wedged between fallen stones. Magnus suppressed a shudder and exchanged a glance with Vigdís. Ancient bones should be less disconcerting than a warm dead body. Somehow this one wasn't.

'Have you any idea how old it is?' Vigdís asked Edda.

'Not yet. Could be anything from two years to two hundred years. Or older, I suppose.'

'Who found it?' Magnus asked the sergeant.

'Two German tourists. They alerted the farmer and he called it in.'

'And where are they?'

'Back at the farm. Selvík. It's just near the turn-off on the fjord road. You passed it on your way here.'

'OK. Let's go and talk to them.'

Selvík's small kitchen was crowded: Magnus, Vigdís, a female officer from Akranes, the two German tourists and the farmer. They could only just fit around the kitchen table.

The kitchen was simple but clean, and warm. An ancient iron range dominated one wall. A couple of intricately worked framed tapestries – images of the farmhouse itself and some pink roses – looked down upon the bright blue-and-white-checked cloth that covered the table.

Magnus noticed a flicker of movement at the doorway: a wrinkled grey head appeared and disappeared just as quickly. The creator of the needlework, no doubt.

Magnus started in English with the German couple, Heinrich Lang and Bettina Franke. Theirs was the rented Toyota that Magnus had seen by the turn-off at Selvík. They had parked to go for a little hike.

'And why did you decide to go into that gully?' Magnus asked.

'Oh. It looked interesting,' said the man. Magnus noticed his girlfriend shift uncomfortably.

The farmer, Jón, snorted. 'That place is dangerous.'

'Tell us how you found the skull?'

'Um. I was taking a photo of Bettina and she noticed it. She screamed. We ran off to get help.'

Magnus glanced at Bettina. These people were hiding something. What?

'Did you take her photograph with your phone?' Magnus said.

The German nodded calmly.

'May I see it?'

His girlfriend stiffened.

'I'd rather not show it to you,' Heinrich said, equally calmly.

'I'd like to see it.'

Heinrich glanced at his girlfriend. 'Don't you need a warrant?'

Magnus managed to stop himself from smiling. 'Technically, we do. And I can get one, if you wish. The very fact you are reluctant to show us the picture makes me suspicious and I know a judge will agree.'

'Then get a warrant. My photographs are private.'

Heinrich Lang was a small man, but he managed to project an air of arrogance.

Magnus looked at the woman, whose expression betrayed a tense mixture of embarrassment and irritation.

He felt sorry for her. 'Bettina, would you rather my colleague Vigdís saw the picture? I doubt there is any need for me to take a look.'

The irritation won. The woman turned to her boyfriend and unleashed a tirade of rapid German. His hauteur crumbled, his shoulders slumped and he handed over his phone.

She passed it to Vigdís. 'It was all Heinie's idea,' she muttered angrily.

Vigdís flicked through the photographs, her expression politely serious. She turned to Magnus. 'Naked,' she said in Icelandic. 'She looks cold.'

'I see,' said Magnus with a smile of kindness, rather than amusement. 'It's possible that we may need these as evidence in an inquiry, but it's unlikely. I'll do my best to avoid it if I can. The important thing is you reported it.'

'No wonder Gerdur was upset,' said Jón, in Icelandic.

'Gerdur?'

'Gerdur of Gerdur's Hollow. She's a witch who was buried there three hundred years ago. That's why no one goes in there.'

Magnus raised his eyebrows. You never knew with these farmers how serious they were about the local superstitions that infested the countryside. This one looked serious.

Jón Sigurdsson was a big man in his fifties, with big broad shoulders and a big overhanging belly. His grey hair was long, wispy and unkempt, as was his sandy beard.

'When was the last time you went in there?' Magnus asked.

'Over a year ago. I avoid it if I possibly can. And if I can't, I send in Kappi.'

'Kappi?'

The black-and-white sheepdog pricked up his ears and stuck out his tongue. 'I see,' Magnus said. 'Kappi. And I assume you didn't see anything last year?'

'No. But just looking today, I think there's been another rockfall recently.'

'Another one?'

'Yes. There was a big one about eighty years ago. There used to be a cairn at Gerdur's Hollow, and you were always supposed to add a stone when you went in there. My grandfather forgot once, and a couple of weeks later there was a landslide. The cairn was gone. The whole family has been even more careful since then.'

'I see,' said Magnus.

'Do you think the skull belongs to Gerdur?' the farmer asked. 'Could it be that old?'

'I suppose it could be,' said Magnus. 'We will know soon enough. Although it looks like there are two bodies.'

'Two? I suppose she could have been buried with another witch.'

'Has anyone else gone missing in this neighbourhood?' Vigdís asked. 'More recently? Like in the last couple of years?'

Jón thought. 'Definitely not that recently. There was a Japanese hiker who got lost on Esja about fifteen years ago. But I'm pretty sure they found his body in the end.'

'We can check,' said Vigdís.

'You can ask my mother about Gerdur if you like. Mum!' the farmer called out towards the doorway of the kitchen. 'Mum! Can you talk to the police?'

Within seconds an old lady shuffled into the kitchen.

She was unsteady on her feet, and decades of working on a farm had etched her face, but there was nothing unsteady about her blue eyes. All marbles present and correct.

'Hello,' she said, with a surprisingly sweet smile. 'My name is Frída. I am Jón's mother. I couldn't help overhearing your conversation.'

I bet you couldn't, thought Magnus. The grey head he had seen earlier belonged to this woman.

'Tell them about Gerdur, Mum.'

Magnus glanced at Vigdís. Here we go – full-on elf alert. Magnus was ready for elves, trolls, hidden people, witches, ghosts: whatever the superstitious old lady wanted to throw at him. He would listen politely and then turn the subject back to the twenty-first century.

'Ach, you are such a wuss, Jón. You're as bad as your father. If there ever was a witch called Gerdur, she's long dead and no trouble to any of us.'

Magnus couldn't suppress a grin.

Heinrich rather gallantly got to his feet and the old lady took his seat with another sweet smile. Her bright blue eyes sought out Magnus.

'If you want to know whose bodies those are, they're probably the two people from Laxahóll who disappeared during the war.'

FOUR

August 1940

It was raining. Of course it was bloody raining. It was Iceland.

At least there wasn't much wind. It was the wind that had really got to Lieutenant Tom Marks since he and his men had arrived in Iceland three months earlier.

It would be better once the Nissen huts arrived. These prefabricated dwellings of semi-cylindrical corrugated metal, wood and concrete would keep out the rain and the wind. They even had stoves.

Tom looked out into the gloom at the field of tents that housed his platoon. It was early, 0600. In theory, it was dawn. In practice, black had merged into dark grey. Summer, such as it was, was coming to an end, and it would soon be getting colder. Life was already exceedingly uncomfortable for his men. Unless those Nissen huts came soon, it would get worse than that.

At the outbreak of war, Tom had imagined himself

marching off to France, leading his men in desperate battles against the Hun. Well, there were no Huns in Iceland, at least not yet, but the challenges of leadership in this godforsaken country were many. He was a schoolteacher who had been trained to lead infantrymen, but now he was effectively a foreman on a construction site. Securing supplies took up most of his time, but the most important aspect of his job was keeping up the morale of his men in the face of an implacable and relentless enemy.

The Icelandic weather.

The 49th Division, the 'Polar Bears' as they were now called, had arrived in Iceland in May to relieve the Royal Marines who had initially occupied the island. Tom's platoon was tasked with constructing a defensive position on the southern shore of Hvalfjördur, protecting the new naval base that was being built a few miles further east along the fjord, at Hvammsvík, near its end. His men spent some of their time manning emplacements against Germans who never came. They spent more of their time building and digging things: trenches, pillboxes, anti-aircraft defences, latrines.

The defensive position was a good one, on top of a low hill a hundred yards in from the shoreline. Hvalfjördur was deep, narrow and long, stretching twenty miles inland from Iceland's west coast, protected on either side by great looming mountain ridges. From their position, the platoon's three Vickers heavy machine guns could intercept attackers approaching along the dirt road that ran along the shoreline, or even landing craft attempting to reach Hvammsvík by sea.

The position was known as Tóftir, after the farm that lay a few hundred yards away, and which provided the soldiers with occasional eggs, butter and milk.

Also, possibly, *brennivín*, the 'black death' moonshine made from fermented potato mash and caraway seed that occasionally found its way into the camp. It tasted foul, it was ridiculously strong – much stronger than the army-supplied watered-down rum ration – and most importantly it seemed to spur half of the soldiers who drank it first to exuberance and then to violence. The previous day, Tom had had to put a lance corporal on a charge for fighting.

The work was hard, wet and soul-destroying. But Tom had soon learned that idleness and waiting were even more soul-destroying. Which was why he had been pleased with his commanding officer's plan for a tactical exercise. Tom would leave one section of his platoon defending Tóftir, and take the other two sections in two one-and-a-half-ton lorries up into the hills to eventually link up with the rest of the company from Hvammsvík. The climax of the exercise would be the other two platoons of C Company attacking Tom's defensive position on the crest of a certain hill marked on his map.

The roads were primitive, and the route to their objective involved fording two rivers. The forecast was for more heavy rain. Major Harris wanted to test his company, to see how well they could travel in such difficult conditions. It was best to know what their limitations were before the Germans landed, rather than discover them afterwards.

Tom agreed with the theory but was worried about the rivers. In principle, they became impassable after the snow melted in the spring, but at this time of year at the end of the summer they should be relatively low. Yet there had been an awful lot of rain recently. Tom had discussed it with Major Harris when he was at Hvammsvík planning the exercise, but the major had said that the maps showed they were fordable, and there was only one way to find out if this was the case.

Sergeant Pickersgill told him the lorries were ready, so Tom hopped in beside the driver and they set off.

Even along the road that ran beside the shore, the going was rough as the lorries lurched over potholes in steady rain. But once they turned off the main road on to a smaller gravel track twisting relentlessly uphill, the speed slowed below ten miles an hour as the lorries lurched and bucked. But they were hardy vehicles, well maintained and well driven.

They passed through a rugged landscape of rocks, stone, heather, moss, bilberry bushes and absolutely no trees. A thick grey wall of moisture encircled them. Ahead lay unseen hills; behind an unseen fjord.

They reached the first of the two rivers, which turned out to be little more than a stream, and both lorries crossed it easily. The second was more problematic.

The road ran straight into fast-flowing water, about thirty yards from one bank to the next. Tom, his sergeant and the two drivers got out to take a look.

They were high up in the hills. The ford was positioned at a point where the river took a breather along a shallow valley and broadened out before plunging downwards through rapids just a few yards further down. The water was shallow – a depth of about eighteen inches, which should be manageable – and the riverbed consisted of pebbles rather than sand or mud.

Tom's lorry went first. Corporal Dibb, the driver, took it slow and steady. The lorry shook but made it through. Tom hopped out to watch Sergeant Pickersgill's lorry follow successfully.

But it was still raining.

Tom's platoon reached their objective in the late afternoon, leaving their two lorries at the end of the track and marching the last mile to set up defensive positions on what Tom was pretty sure was the correct hill. According to the map, there was a clear view of the valley from which the rest of the company would be attacking, having made their way up from Hvammsvík by an alternative road.

In practice, Tom could see nothing, just cloud.

Despite the cold and the rain, his men were undaunted. In fact, they almost seemed to be enjoying themselves. At least they weren't digging turf or shifting rocks, and there was a profuse supply of sweet purple bilberries nestling in low bushes right under their noses.

As they stared into the mist, they heard the sound of heavy feet on rock and muffled commands. And a few minutes later they were brewing up with their adversaries and sharing their bilberries.

It was still raining.

The men were wet and tired but in good spirits as they began the long drive back to Tóftir.

Until they came to the river.

The rain had finally stopped, but not before it had swelled the stream. The current had strengthened appreciably and the water was at least a foot deeper.

Once again, Tom, his sergeant and the two drivers dismounted to assess the situation.

It didn't look good.

'What do you think, sir?'

Tom scanned the river. 'We have no choice. I know it's stopped raining, but the water level will only rise from here, so there's no point waiting. And there's no other route back to camp. We have to cross. Do you think you can make it, corporal?'

Dibb grinned. 'Aye, sir. Just as long as we take it steady and don't stop.'

The battalion had been recruited from the West Riding of Yorkshire. Most of the men had worked in the textile mills of Leeds and Bradford; they were small, undernourished but tough. But a few of them, like Dibb, were from the Yorkshire Dales, men who felt at home in the harsh landscape. Before the army, Dibb had spent several years driving a bus up and down Wharfedale in all weathers.

Tom himself had been brought up in North London, although he had attended university in Leeds and taken a job at a prep school at the foot of one of those Yorkshire Dales afterwards. But he certainly wasn't a Dalesman like Dibb.

'Carry on, corporal.'

Dibb did as he had promised, guiding the lorry through the torrent. At one point, close to the far bank, a wheel seemed to slip, but Dibb kept his nerve, easing on and off the accelerator, and they emerged from the river on to the bank.

Sergeant Pickersgill's lorry followed them, slow and steady. It made good progress until it came to the spot where Dibb's wheels had spun and it came to a stop.

The driver revved the engine, and the lorry sank alarmingly to one side.

'Bugger!' said Dibb.

'You're dead right there,' said Tom.

Each lorry was equipped with a tow rope, chains and duckboards. The occupants of the second vehicle jumped out, swearing at the freezing water, and Sergeant Pickersgill organized the tow rope. The water reached up to the men's thighs and they struggled to maintain their footing. Tom was concerned that if one of them fell they might get swept away, but they had to get the vehicle out of the river somehow.

The tow rope didn't work. The next step was to try to insert the duckboards under the rear tyres underwater, and then shove from behind and pull from the front.

That wasn't working either.

Tom began to wish that he had left the lorries on the bank and marched his men across. They had a wireless set and could have called for help from Hvammsvík. It would have taken hours to arrive, but at least he wouldn't have lost a lorry.

Corporal Dibb had an idea. Try placing the duckboards behind the rear wheels of the lorry and push the vehicle backwards on to them. Then drive forwards out of the river.

Tom was doubtful, but it was worth a try.

Four men waded out to move the duckboards. One of them was Private Sowerby. He was a mill worker from one of the Halifax carpet factories. He was thin, and not much over five feet tall.

'I say, will Sowerby be all right, sergeant?' Tom asked.

'Oh, he'll be fine,' said the sergeant. 'He's not big, but he's a strong lad.'

Tom knew Sowerby was tough, and brave too. He was popular with the other men, but a bit of a troublemaker. He had, of course, been involved in the *brennivín* incident the other night, but he had by all accounts broken the resulting fight up.

A good man to have in a tight spot.

The water was rising noticeably and the current seemed to be strengthening, especially farther out in the river. It was almost up to Sowerby's waist.

Moving the duckboards involved stooping down into the freezing water. But the men were determined, and within ten minutes they had successfully placed the boards behind the rear wheels.

Dibb took the place of the driver in the second vehicle, and Tom plunged into the river with the rest of his platoon. The cold took his breath away, seeping through his woollen trousers and into his boots. He joined the back of what was now essentially a rugby scrum, leaning against the bonnet of the lorry.

At the count of three, Dibb revved the engine in reverse and the men pushed.

The lorry rocked, but nothing.

They tried again. This time the vehicle budged. Then it budged some more.

'The wagon's on the boards!' shouted Sowerby, still at the back.

The soldiers dispersed. Dibb revved the accelerator, put the engine into gear, and the lorry lurched forward. And it kept going.

A loud cheer rose from the men.

With the water still swirling around his thighs, Tom looked further out into the river, where the four soldiers who had moved the duckboard were joining in with the cheering. Sowerby raised his arms in triumph, grinning at his mates, and then he swayed backwards, stumbled and fell.

The current sent him tumbling downstream.

Tom turned and scrambled for the bank. He sprinted along the side of the river, watching as Sowerby's body rushed off ahead of him. Sowerby had managed to wrest his head above water, but the current, already fast, was speeding up as the river entered a narrower rocky channel before hurrying around a bend and out of sight.

As Tom ran he had no idea how far the rapids lasted. Maybe there was a quieter patch just around the bend.

Or a waterfall. He thought he could hear a distant roar.

There was no quiet patch, just rocks. But Sowerby was clinging to one of them, his arms hanging on to a small boulder in the middle of the stream, his legs dangling behind him in the water.

Tom could not let Private Sowerby die.

He was responsible for him. He could have abandoned the lorries on the bank and marched the platoon across the river. He could have insisted that Sowerby make way for a larger man behind the second lorry.

If he had done either of those things, Sowerby would not be clinging on to a boulder in the midst of a freezing torrent.

Gingerly, Tom stepped off the bank into the fast-running water. It reached up to his waist and tugged him down. It was only by holding on to an overhanging bush that he stopped himself from being swept away. The cold tore through his legs and his groin, leaving him gasping. He began to shake.

Sowerby was only five yards away. But Tom couldn't reach him.

He knew it. Sowerby stared at him, fear in his eyes, and shook his head.

Sowerby knew it too.

Tom looked downstream. About thirty yards down, the river narrowed further, splitting into two around a large boulder. The left channel passed close to the bank. The right channel didn't.

About twenty yards beyond that, the river just disappeared into air.

A waterfall.

'Hold on, Sowerby!' Tom cried. 'Just hold on!'

Tom scrambled back up the bank, and clambered over the rocks along the edge of the river until he came to the point where the current parted.

Here there was a large boulder jammed against the bank which broke the flow. He waded out in relatively calm water behind it to the edge of the channel running by the rock in the middle of the river. The channel was about six feet across and flowing very fast.

Tom looked upstream. It was impossible to judge whether if Sowerby let go he would be swept into the left channel or the right. He *might* go left. Or he might not.

There was no other choice.

Tom found as firm a footing as he could against rocks on the riverbed and yelled upstream: 'Let go, Sowerby!'

Sowerby's face was pale, but determined – no sign of panic. He nodded.

He let go.

Immediately he was swept away downstream.

Sowerby managed to keep his head above water, and he splashed and kicked in an attempt to steer himself to the left.

For a moment it looked as if he would be swept right. Tom didn't know if it was just luck or Sowerby's kicks, but at the last instant his body swirled along the left channel, spinning as it did so.

Tom only had one chance to catch him; if he missed, Sowerby would hurtle past him and over the waterfall. Tom reached out and grabbed an arm, twisting Sowerby's light body away from the centre of the current and towards the bank.

But as he did so, Tom lost his own footing. His head

went under. He writhed and kicked down against the riverbed with his right leg.

Fortunately, his foot made purchase against a rock. He pushed hard against the current, and scrabbled around with his other leg for a foothold.

He found one. With all his strength he forced himself through the water to the calm eddy behind the boulder at the river's edge, where he collapsed next to Sowerby.

Strong arms pulled both of them out on to the bank.

He found himself looking up at the ruddy face of Sergeant Pickersgill.

'That were bloody stupid, sir,' the sergeant said with a grin.

Tom was shaking uncontrollably with cold, but he managed a smile. 'Carry on, sergeant.'

FIVE

The Nissen huts arrived, together with winter clothing – boots with rubber covers and wool insoles, warm socks, leather mittens with wool liners – and a delayed bundle of letters. A bag of seven footballs and seven rugger balls appeared; only the army knew why a platoon of thirty men needed fourteen balls, especially since they didn't have enough .303 rounds for the Vickers machine guns. They even received new shoulder patches: an image of the division's new emblem, a rather glum polar bear. Morale rose, particularly once the first delivery of coke was received for the Nissen huts' stoves.

It stopped raining. For the first time in weeks, Tom's platoon was dry.

No sign of the Germans, apart from a lone Focke-Wulf 200 that had flown high overhead one afternoon to great excitement. The codeword 'Julius' would mean an attack from the air or sea was taking place, 'Caesar' that German soldiers had landed. Fortunately, they had heard nothing from the Roman Emperor. However, an impressive-looking anti-aircraft gun arrived – with its attendant searchlight – to take up its position in the emplacement the men had prepared for it, together with a detachment of Royal Artillery to pamper it.

In addition to the lorries, the platoon had also been equipped with two motorcycles, Royal Enfield 350 ccs. Tom commandeered one of these. He had owned a smaller BSA Blue Star back in England, which he had used to ride around the Yorkshire countryside from the prep school at which he was teaching.

After the problems on the last tactical exercise, Tom wanted to confirm for himself the quality of the roads and any river crossings in the region. But he also wanted to get away from the camp and explore the countryside alone.

He set off along the road that ran along the southern edge of Hvalfjördur. The sun was shining, glinting off the fjord's deep waters. A sleek destroyer lurked at anchor. Behind that, a wall of steep hills rose from the far shore. It was hard to believe that these were the same hills that for the last month had glowered black and grey across dark waters to the camp. On his left stood the mighty bulk of Esja, which formed a formidable barrier between the Whale Fjord and Reykjavík to the south-west. A barely perceptible pale half-disk of moon hovered in the blue sky ahead.

Autumn had arrived in Iceland. The grass on the hill-sides shimmered golden in the sunlight and the leaves of the squat bushes beside the road had turned yellow and crim-son. It was more subtle than an English wood in October, but just as beautiful.

He opened the Enfield's throttle and felt the cool air and the timid yellow sunshine on his cheeks. His spirits rose.

As part of his English degree at Leeds University, Tom

had studied Old Norse, as well as Anglo-Saxon. So he knew that Hvalfjördur meant Whale Fjord. He had yet to see one, though, and he hadn't heard of a sighting yet, but he always kept an eye out for a whale spout just in case.

When he came to Selvík – Seal Bay – he stopped. An old farm made of stone and turf, with a roof upon which thick grass grew, stood just back from the road by a turning. A ribbon of smoke twisted upwards from the central chimney, and Tom could smell peat.

The dwelling looked damp and cold, more like a burrow than a house. But presumably the farm animals and the fire kept it warm.

Out in the fjord, he saw a head break the water's surface and a seal stared at him, like a curious dog. Then it was gone.

He turned inland along a well-maintained gravel road beside a clear river, the Selá – Seal River. The river valley was narrow for a stretch, then it turned and opened out into a broad area of lush green fields. Horses grazed, as did some extremely woolly sheep and a dozen or so cattle. They were Icelandic breeds, smaller than their English equivalents, and they came in a variety of colours. The horses watched his motorbike curiously under long fringes of mane; the sheep and the cows seemed less impressed.

He approached a farm, more prosperous than Selvík, which he knew from his map was called Laxahóll – Salmon Hill. That was interesting. Tom had bought a rod on his last visit to Reykjavík and was hopeful of finding somewhere to use it. He had learned to fly fish while teaching at the school in Yorkshire, which had been situated only half a mile from a good trout stream.

Unlike Selvík, this farmhouse was constructed of white concrete with a red metal roof, although the barns next to it were made of the traditional stone and turf. Not far behind it stood a small white metal church.

Chickens scurried about by the roadside. A woman and a boy were feeding them from a bucket. The woman was tall and red-haired and had quite a figure. She smiled, nudged the boy and pointed to Tom on his bike. Tom waved and the small boy waved back, as did the woman. He noticed that she didn't wear her hair long and plaited, like most of the women in the countryside Tom had seen, but rather collar length and curled like the girls at home.

The road was comparatively well maintained, but this was Iceland, so there was a pothole, and with his eyes off the road, Tom and his motorcycle found it. The front wheel bucked and twisted and slid, and Tom went over the handlebars. He wasn't wearing a helmet. He managed to duck his head in time so that his skull only sustained a glancing blow.

He lay on the ground, stunned, but still conscious.

The woman squatted next to him, her concerned expression only a few inches from his face.

He closed his eyes and shook his head. 'Ouch,' he said.

She said something in Icelandic. He raised his goggles and tried to focus. He had been teaching himself Icelandic over the last few months, with the help of a dictionary and his Old Norse.

She repeated it. 'Are you all right?'

'Yes,' said Tom. 'I am just stupid.'

This made her laugh. 'You speak Icelandic?'

'No.'

Tom pulled himself to his feet and held his head and his shoulder. He flexed his arm. It hurt, but it wasn't broken.

He couldn't believe what an idiot he had been. Ogling a girl and driving right into a pothole.

'I see if my . . . if my . . .'

The woman raised her eyebrows.

He searched for the word he was looking for, but gave up – it was beyond his Old Norse. 'If my iron stallion is good.'

She laughed. 'Iron stallion?'

'Yes. It is a kenning. You know kennings?'

Kennings were the phrases that Norsemen used in the sagas to describe honoured objects. One that Tom had always liked was 'falcon perch', which meant arm. A ship was a 'surge horse', which is probably where Tom got the idea for iron stallion.

'Oh, yes, of course.'

'So what do you call that in Icelandic?' Tom asked, pointing to the motorcycle, splayed out on the edge of the road.

'I think I will call it iron stallion from now on,' said the woman. 'Can Gudni stroke your iron stallion?'

'Of course.' Gudni was a small boy with fair hair and big, big blue eyes. Tom took him by the hand and led him to the iron stallion. Tom picked it up from the dirt and examined it. It looked all right, as far as he could tell.

'Do you want to mount the stallion?'

The boy nodded, and Tom lifted him on to the seat, wincing as he did so.

'Your head is bleeding,' said the woman. 'Here, let me take a look.'

Tom was happy to bow his head to let her run her fingers through his army-cut hair.

'Blood. Look.' She showed him her fingers, and they were indeed red.

'Beer of wounds,' said Tom.

'Well, just make sure you don't drink it,' said the

woman. 'Come into the farm and I will wash it and bandage it.' At least that's what Tom thought she said – he was guessing the 'bandage' bit.

As he followed her and the boy up the slope to the door of the farmhouse, a sprightly man in his fifties approached them from one of the turf barns. He wasn't very tall, but he looked strong. He sported a well-trimmed, pointed beard – red with streaks of grey – and a classic Icelandic jersey of an intricate blue and white pattern.

'This my father, Hálfdán,' said the woman. 'This is a British soldier who was charging our farm on his iron stallion. He fell off.'

'Cavalry, eh,' said the man, with a twinkle in his blue eyes. 'A battle wound, I see.'

The woman said something in Icelandic that was too rapid for Tom to follow, and led him into the farmhouse, indicating that he should take off his boots.

The kitchen was spotless and looked as modern as its British equivalent, although better decorated, with photographs of family members ancient and modern, paintings of landscapes and blue and yellow curtains. A stove kept the room deliciously warm. The woman turned on a tap at the sink and hot water miraculously appeared – Tom hadn't seen a tap do that for a while. She filled a bowl, took a sponge and dabbed at Tom's hair.

'What's your name?' she asked.

'Tom.' He was aware that Icelanders tended to use first names even in polite conversation. Especially in polite conversation. 'And yours?'

'Kristín. And this is my son Gudni.'

'Hello, Gudni.'

'How do you speak Icelandic?'

'I learned Old Norse at university in England. And I

have tried to pick up modern Icelandic since I have been here.'

'You are doing well, although your accent is terrible.'

'No, it's not.'

'Yes, it is.'

'This is how the Vikings spoke.'

Kristín leaned back. 'That's ridiculous.'

'How do you know?'

'How do *you* know?'

'I learned it from my professor.'

'And he was a Viking?'

'Maybe. His name was Tolkien. That sounds Viking to me.'

'Not to me. Here. Hold this against your head and I'll get you some coffee.'

The old farmer pulled a small silver box from his pocket. After offering it to Tom, who shook his head, he extracted a pinch of snuff, threw back his head, snorted several times and then blew his nose loudly on a handkerchief. He smiled with triumph at his performance and again offered the box to Tom, clearly perplexed as to why he wouldn't want to join in.

Coffee arrived, with plenty of cream, and delicious pastries, in which cinnamon played a big part. As Tom drank and ate, his head cleared. His two hosts were eager to talk to him. Tom dug his Icelandic–English dictionary out of his pocket and did the best he could. He had had some conversational practice with the farmer at Tóftir and with some of the Icelandic workmen who had been drafted in near company HQ at Hvammsvík to build the naval facilities. He found the farmer Hálfdán difficult to understand – he spoke in short sharp bursts where the words tumbled over each other. But Kristín was much easier to follow. She spoke slowly and clearly, and seemed to know when to be patient and wait or repeat herself.

Tom wasn't bad at languages. He had studied English, German and Latin at his own school in North London, and was even responsible for teaching the Lower Fourth Latin at the Yorkshire prep school. Although many of the words were similar to English, Icelandic – and Old Norse for that matter – were even more difficult than Latin grammatically.

The farmer seemed to enjoy pointing out Tom's many mistakes; Kristín was kinder.

Tom surreptitiously scanned the family photographs. There was one of a younger Hálfdán with a light-haired woman in a wedding dress who was a couple of inches taller than him and looked a lot like Kristín. Her mother, no doubt.

There was another photo of Kristín and a young, devilishly good-looking man in a suit. Her husband.

Oh, well. The woman had a son, so she was bound to have a husband.

Tom was enjoying himself, as were his hosts. But after an hour or so, he looked at his watch. 'I must go. I should be back at the camp before it gets dark.'

'Why? Can't your iron stallion see in the dark?' Kristín asked.

'Of course it can!' said her father. 'It's got that giant light on it.'

'It probably could,' Tom admitted.

'Stay for supper then,' Hálfdán said.

'Yes, stay,' said Kristín. 'Siggi will be home soon; in fact, he is late. Why don't you show Tom the farm, Dad, while I get supper ready?'

So, Hálfdán showed Tom his farm. It was indeed large and prosperous. He proudly showed off a Massey

Ferguson tractor, and a gleaming black Model T, although it was clear that the farm's horses still did most of the work and the transport. Electricity came from a little generator over a small waterfall a hundred yards up the hillside. There were barns made of turf for storing hay and sheltering animals, and even one for drying the down from the eider ducks that nested about the farm. A wooden smoking hut for salmon and lamb stood next to a small stone smithy for making and fixing tools. Chickens, geese and two sheepdogs clucked, strutted and sniffed about the farm.

About a hundred yards away, and a little up the hillside, stood the tiny church, low sunshine glinting off its white metal walls. Tom's military eye picked it out as a good position from which to command the valley.

'Let me show you the river.'

The Selá swayed in an easy rhythm as it passed the farm, green meadows on either side.

The water was clear, the current steady.

'Salmon?' Tom asked.

'Yes,' said the farmer. He then said another word that Tom didn't understand, but after a couple of repetitions and rapid leafing through his dictionary, Tom realized he meant 'trout'.

Tom peered into the water in vain. The farmer beckoned him, and together they crouched low and crept along the bank until they crawled on to a boulder and peeked over.

Sure enough, there were three lovely salmon, facing upstream, shimmering a couple of inches underwater, their tails flickering in the current.

Tom heard the sound of hooves and turned to see a small man on a horse trot up along the road from Selvík – it wasn't exactly a trot, more the smooth rapid Icelandic gait known as a tölt.

Hálfdán waved. The man on the horse acknowledged him, dismounted and removed the saddle and bridle.

'Siggi?' Tom asked.

Hálfdán nodded.

'Kristín's husband?'

This seemed to strike Hálfdán as very funny indeed. Tom waited, feeling foolish.

'Sigurdur is only eighteen. He is Kristín's younger brother. I have another son who is studying abroad at the moment.'

'Oh, I see. Where is her husband?' Tom scanned the farm buildings.

Hálfdán stopped laughing. 'He died. In Reykjavík. Two years ago. And then my wife died last year. So Kristín came back to Laxahóll with little Gudni.'

'Oh, I am sorry.' And Tom was. Any momentary relief that Kristín was unattached was quickly squashed by sympathy for the two of them. 'It is good you can help each other.'

'Yes,' Hálfdán said. 'My wife would be pleased that Kristín came back. But I worry that she is getting bored.'

The blue eyes recovered their twinkle. 'Come in. She is a very good cook.'

Supper was cold – delicious dark red smoked lamb on rye bread with some cheese. And skyr and berries for pudding – skyr being a cross between curd cheese and yoghurt.

Siggi was small and dark but looked a strong fellow. Physically, he reminded Tom of Private Sowerby, although he was a lot less cheerful. In fact, he was a thoroughly sullen youth. Tom wasn't impressed, and his sister and father seemed embarrassed.

'Siggi is going to start *Bretavinnan* next week,' Kristín said. 'At the new naval base.'

'Oh, yes,' said Tom. He knew *Bretavinnan* meant work for the British.

Siggi didn't seem particularly enthused by the idea.

'It's well paid,' said Hálfdán. Tom managed to suppress a smile. The Icelandic labourers at the naval base had been complaining and even threatening to strike because they were being paid less than their compatriots in Reykjavík.

'I will look out for you next time I am there,' said Tom.

Siggi grunted.

After dinner was over, Tom once again took his leave.

'Please come again,' said Hálfdán.

'Yes, do come,' said Kristín.

'Do you like to fish?' Hálfdán asked.

Tom beamed. 'Yes, I do. In fact, I recently bought myself a rod.'

'Well, you are welcome to fish here.'

'That is very kind,' said Tom.

'Shouldn't he pay?' said Siggi.

Hálfdán looked at his son sharply. Undercutting his father's hospitality didn't go down well.

But Kristín took her brother's side. 'Yes, absolutely he should pay. That way he can come as often as he likes.'

Hálfdán raised his eyebrows. Tom sort of followed her logic: if he paid, he wouldn't have to wait for an invitation. That implied that Kristín wanted him to come again. More than once.

Siggi looked at her in something close to horror.

Kristín appeared momentarily confused, as if she had just said something she didn't mean to, but then she brazened it out. She suggested a price. Tom counter-offered. There was a little haggling and then the deal was done.

Tom left the farm on his iron stallion, gingerly guiding it around the potholes in the dark until he reached the fjord. Pale moonlight laid a shimmering yellow path towards him over its deep waters. The sky above the mountains to the north was tinged with shimmering green brushstrokes of northern lights.

He realized he was grinning, and he let out a loud whoop on the empty road, just because he felt like it.

SIX

September 2023

'Two people disappeared from Laxahóll?' said Magnus. 'That's the farm just up the road, isn't it?'

'That's right,' Frída, the old lady, said. 'It caused a huge fuss. It was a few years before I was born – I think at the beginning of the war – but people round here were still talking about it when I was growing up.'

'And who were these two?'

'A brother and a sister. Marteinn Hálfdánsson and his sister Kristín.'

'Were they children? How old were they?'

'Oh, no, they were adults. In fact, Kristín was a widow with a young son. I think Marteinn was younger. No one knows what happened. There were a lot of British soldiers and sailors around here during the war, and some people said it had something to do with them. But it was a mystery.'

'Did the police investigate?'

'I assume so. I don't know. But they must have done, mustn't they? And perhaps the British Army as well?'

'You don't know it's them, Mum,' said Jón. 'It could be Gerdur.'

The old woman ignored him, as did Magnus and Vigdís.

'Does that family still own Laxahóll?' Vigdís asked.

'Oh, no. They sold up in the 1970s. And then the people who bought it sold it on to some folks from Reykjavík.'

'There's a high-end fishing lodge there now,' said Jón. 'The Selá is good for salmon. They charge a fortune.' He shrugged. 'Laxahóll has always had the fishing rights on the river, even for the stretch that runs by Selvík.'

'What about descendants? Are any of the family left?'

'Well, there's Jón,' said Frída, nodding towards her son, the farmer. 'There was another brother, Sigurdur, who I married. He came to farm here. He's Jón's father.'

Magnus raised his eyebrows. 'So that means you were quite a bit younger than him?'

'Oh, yes. I was only nineteen when I married Siggi, and he was in his forties. He was married himself at the time.' She sighed. 'I suppose I should feel guilty, but at nineteen Siggi really turned my head, and he would have left his wife anyway.'

'Divorce happens,' said Jón gruffly. 'My father was a good man.' He glared at Magnus as he said this, as if daring the detective to contradict him.

'He was indeed,' said Frída, with a smile. She fetched a photograph from the dresser. It was a colour picture of a pretty young blonde woman with a small dark-haired man almost twice her age. He had a roguish smile. 'That's him,' she said. 'And me.'

'Did your families fall out over this?' Vigdís asked.

'I'll say,' said Frída. 'Siggi was kicked out of Laxahóll and came to farm with my family here. With no heir to take over the farm apart from Gudni, Hálfdán sold out and moved to Borgarnes. He died pretty soon after. That's why we don't really know the details of Marteinn and Kristín's disappearance.'

'And who is Gudni?' Magnus asked.

'Gudni was Kristín's little boy. I told you she was a widow.'

'What happened to him?'

'He stayed on at Laxahóll after she died. Siggi and Hálfdán and Siggi's first wife looked after him. But he wasn't interested in farming. He became an engineer.'

'Do you know if he is still alive?'

'Yes, or at least he was last Christmas. He sends us a Christmas card every year. I can get you his address. Somewhere in Grafarholt, I think.'

'That would be very helpful,' said Magnus.

'I can also give you the address of an Englishwoman who came over here a few years ago. She was asking about Kristín. She said her father had known her during the war and had told her all about her. She was a nice lady.'

Frída turned to her son. 'You remember her, don't you, love? Jón had to do the translation,' she explained. 'I don't speak English, but he does.'

'I do remember her,' said Jón. 'She came here one afternoon – I'd say in 2017. She seemed to know all about Laxahóll, but when she went up there to ask them questions, they sent her down here. Not that we could be of any help.'

'As I said, all this happened several years before I was born in 1945,' the old woman added.

'Did your husband say much about the disappearances?' Vigdís asked.

'No,' said Frída. 'It upset him too much. It made him angry.'

'I assume he has passed away now?' said Magnus.

'Oh, yes. Twenty years ago. He would be a hundred and one now! Let me get those addresses.'

She shuffled off out of the kitchen, and returned a minute later with a dog-eared address book and read out an address for Gudni Thorsteinsson in Grafarholt, and for the Englishwoman, whose name was Louisa Sugarman, as well as an email address.

Magnus and Vigdís were just about to leave when Magnus's phone rang.

'Hi, Edda. What have you got?'

'We've found the other skull. And you know what?'

'Tell me.'

'It has a bullet hole in it.'

SEVEN

'Now, are you sure you don't want to stop and interview some hidden people?' Vigdís said with a grin as they were driving along the side of the fjord back to Reykjavík. 'For a moment there I thought we were back in Bolungarvík. Same MO.'

Several years before, Magnus had been involved in a case in the West Fjords, where someone had been killed in a landslide and the locals had been adamant that the hidden people had done it, hidden people being invisible inhabitants of the Icelandic countryside with special powers.

'I liked that old woman,' Magnus said. 'Refreshingly down to earth. Unlike her son.'

'Do you want me to check missing persons?'

'Not yet. Hopefully, Edda will soon be able to give us a steer on which century we're looking at.'

'Or find the bullet that killed them,' Vigdís said. 'Shall we check out the Laxahóll brother and sister?'

'Yes. Let's go and see that Gudni now. And I'll send the Englishwoman an email – see if she can shed a light on things.'

Magnus was driving along the edge of Hvalfjördur. 'It's hard to imagine now, but you know this fjord was crammed with Allied ships during the war?' he said. 'They used this as a staging point for the Arctic convoys to Russia. And as a base for attacking German U-boats.'

Vigdís groaned. 'Time for another history lecture. I didn't know you did World War Two as well as the sagas.'

'I'm just saying there would have been a lot of British servicemen around here. And Americans after 1941. Although if the brother and sister were killed at the beginning of the war, that would be before most of the facilities were built.'

Vigdís was about to reply when her phone chirped. 'Hi, Olla . . . What? . . . Are you sure? . . . Is Erla OK? . . . I'm coming home right now.'

'What is it?' said Magnus.

'My neighbour. She saw Mum tip over the pushchair when she took Erla outside. She thinks she's drunk.'

Magnus put his foot down.

Vigdís lived in Hafnarfjördur, a fishing port about fifteen kilometres on the other side of Reykjavík from Hvalfjördur. As she battled through the traffic, conflicting thoughts swirled around her brain. Why had she let Mum look after Erla? Was Erla really OK? How long had Mum been drinking? Why, oh why had she let her near the baby?

She always knew it would be difficult being a single mother. If you were well organized – and Vigdís was – everything was all right as long as everyone did what they were supposed to do. But as soon as something went wrong – like Erla getting a cold so she couldn't go to day care, for example – Vigdís was left in a panic, scrambling just to get through the day.

If she had a partner, things would be easier. But although Vigdís knew who Erla's father was, he had no idea he had a daughter, and Vigdís wanted to keep it that way.

Her flat was on the second floor of a modern four-storey apartment block not far from the busy harbour. She ran up the stairs and threw open the door. Erla was watching *PAW Patrol* on TV in the living room, her grandmother, Audur, sitting next to her.

'Ah, you're home, love.'

Vigdís rushed over to her daughter, picked her up and squeezed her. The little girl giggled. 'Ow!' she protested, but she didn't mean it.

Vigdís put her down on the armchair away from her grandmother.

Audur was smiling up at her. She was small and pale, with short, stringy blonde hair, a tiny pert nose and a pointed chin. 'You're back early. What's wrong, love?'

Vigdís bent down and inhaled. 'You smell of gin!'

'No, I do not,' said Audur, attempting another unsteady grin.

Vigdís went into the kitchen. The bottle of red wine was still there. But not the three-quarters-full bottle of gin.

'Where is it?' she demanded.

'Where is what?'

'The gin bottle.'

'What gin bottle?'

Erla giggled, pointed at the corner of the sofa and said: 'Bottle.'

Vigdís hurled the cushion on to the floor. There was the bottle, nearly empty.

She picked it up and waved it at her mother. 'Mum! How could you?'

Erla started to cry. Vigdís ignored her.

'It wasn't me,' said Audur unconvincingly. 'You must have left it there.'

'Don't be ridiculous, Mum. I'm not letting you near my child alone ever again, do you understand?'

Her mother's face crumpled. 'Oh, please, Vigdís,' she said, a tear leaking from an eye. 'I only had a small drink.'

'The bottle was nearly full!'

Audur began to sob.

'Go!' Vigdís pointed to the door. Erla was screaming now.

'Vigdís, please.'

'I said go! And don't drive home.' Audur lived in Keflavík, thirty kilometres away. 'I'm going to call a cab. Go downstairs and wait for it outside the front door.'

'Vigdís?'

'Now!'

Audur bent to say goodbye to Erla, but Vigdís snatched her daughter away. 'Now!'

Audur took her bag and left the apartment. Vigdís whipped out her phone and, still holding a weeping Erla, called a local taxi company. They said they could have someone pick up her mother outside the building in five minutes.

Vigdís shushed Erla and tried to get her settled in front of the TV. She was angry at her mother, but she was angrier at herself. She wondered when Audur had started drinking again. Maybe she had never really stopped?

What an idiot Vigdís had been! And she had left the bottle of gin out in the kitchen. That was dumb too.

She went over to the window to look for the taxi. It

hadn't arrived yet, but she saw Audur climb into her silver Kia, parked on the side street in front of Vigdís's apartment block. Vigdís banged on the window, but her mother couldn't hear her.

The Kia reversed rapidly and then drove off.

Right into a jogger.

He was a tall man in his twenties. He had been crossing the quiet street. His body was tossed over the bonnet.

Vigdís put her hand to her mouth and let out a yelp.

The Kia stopped briefly. And then accelerated away.

Vigdís grabbed Erla and sprinted out of her flat and down the stairs. She ran out into the road to the man.

He was lying on the street, his face pressed to the ground, blood dribbling out of his nose. His eyes were closed. He was wearing earbuds; Vigdís eased one of them out of his ear. A podcast was still playing, a tinny murmur.

'Are you OK?'

No response. He was out cold. But not dead. Probably not dead.

Vigdís dialled 112 and demanded an ambulance. She knew they would send a police car as well, but she didn't ask for that. Thankfully, Erla seemed bemused, not distressed: she didn't understand what was happening.

A couple of passers-by joined her. He was still breathing! She was sure he was still breathing.

His eyes flickered as he came round. He winced. 'Oww.'

He tried to get up but winced some more. 'Stay there,' said Vigdís. 'The ambulance will be here in a minute.'

But sure enough, it was a police car which arrived first, Lúdvík and María from the Hafnarfjördur police station.

'Hi, Vigdís,' said Lúdvík. 'What happened?'

'Hit and run,' said Vigdís, without thinking.

'Did you see it?'

'Not directly. I live just up there and I was looking out of the window. I didn't really see it.'

'And they didn't stop?'

'Drove right off,' said Vigdís. 'I think the vehicle was silver. Small. Don't know the make. As I said, I didn't really see it.'

'Did any of you see anything?' Lúdvík asked the small crowd of people that had gathered to gawk.

They all shook their heads as first the taxi and then the ambulance arrived. Within a couple of minutes, the jogger was on his way to hospital.

And Vigdís realized she had just lied to the police.

EIGHT

October 1940

Tom tried to get back to Laxahóll as often as he could, but it wasn't often enough. He had no one overseeing him, apart from Major Harris at company headquarters five miles away at Hvammsvík, but there was always a lot to be done at Tóftir, and it was hard to get away.

The first time he had returned, it was with his rod. Hálfdán had enthusiastically shown him the river and watched as he cast. To Tom's delight, he caught three fine salmon.

The farmer invited him back to the farmhouse for coffee and cake, served by Kristín, who seemed pleased to see him, as was Gudni. Hálfdán did most of the talking – he clearly liked to talk – with Kristín helping out, repeating his sentences more slowly and clearly, while he took the opportunity to snort some snuff. Tom had never heard anyone sneeze so loudly.

The next week, Tom arrived with one of the platoon's

many footballs for Gudni, who was ecstatic. Tom explained that the best football team in the entire world was called Spurs, and the best player in the world was called Willie Hall. Gudni absorbed this information earnestly, much to his mother and grandfather's amusement.

Tom had also brought his camera, a Brownie, and took half a dozen snaps of the farm, of Hálfdán, of Gudni. And of Kristín.

There was no sign of Siggi – he was now working on the construction team at the naval base – earning good money, according to his father.

Tom didn't miss him.

As he took his leave, Kristín walked out to his motorbike with him.

'Is there room on your iron stallion for two?' she asked. 'It looks fun.'

'It is,' Tom said. 'Jump on.'

'What, now? I thought you had to get back to your camp?'

Tom did. But bugger it. 'That's all right. We'll go to the mouth of the fjord and back. Won't take long.'

'All right.'

Tom started off at a steady pace along the shore road, intensely aware of Kristín's arms clinging to his waist.

'Doesn't this horse gallop any faster?'

He opened the throttle. The fjord whizzed by as the bike juddered and bucked over the gravel road. They overtook a convoy of three British trucks, fortunately not from his company. In no time they had reached the mouth of the fjord; a pair of corvettes was steaming towards them from the west, fresh from escorting a convoy across the Atlantic. Tom continued, and in a few minutes more they had rounded the headland to the next fjord, Kollafjördur.

He pulled over and he and Kristín dismounted. Her face was flushed and excited.

A cloud stepped back from the sun, which streamed across the small fjord. They perched on a rock by the road, low bushes of red and yellow gathered about their feet. There was a faint smell of fish, presumably emanating from the racks drying cod a hundred yards distant. Tom had noticed there was often a faint smell of fish in the most unlikely places in Iceland. And sulphur.

Behind them rose a steep wall of stone, topped by a dusting of snow, a mountain Tom knew well from his maps as Esja. Over the fjord, about five miles distant, a jumble of metal buildings clustered around a hill. Ships large and small buzzed around the harbour.

Reykjavík.

Tom reached into his battledress and pulled out his faithful, much-thumbed dictionary.

Kristín glanced down at it. 'I do like that book.'

'Why?'

'Because whenever you take it out you want to talk to me.'

Tom glanced at her, unsure of what to make of her comment. Her expression didn't give anything away.

Then she smiled. 'Does it have a name?'

'Of course not. Why should it have a name?'

'We should give it a name.' She looked out to sea for inspiration. 'I know! Ari. As in Ari the Learned. Have you heard of him?'

'Wasn't he the first chap to write Iceland's history in Old Norse?'

'That's right. Iceland's first scholar. Here, do you have a pen?'

'I have a pencil. An officer cannot fight a war without a pencil.' He handed it to her.

She took the pencil and the dictionary and scribbled something in it. Tom read it and chuckled.

He looked up at the small city. 'You used to live there, didn't you?'

'Yes. With Thorsteinn.'

'Your father said he died a couple of years ago. I am sorry.'

'He was run over by a car. He was crossing a road. Stupid driver didn't know what he was doing.'

The levity had gone. Her expression was a mixture of sadness and bitterness. But Tom didn't regret bringing up the subject. He knew he couldn't understand her unless he knew about her husband. And he wanted to understand her.

'How did you meet him?'

'In Copenhagen. I went there to study for a year – many Icelanders do. My brother Marteinn is there now, or at least I think he is. Thorsteinn was studying there too. His family comes from Reykjavík; his father is a merchant there. We fell in love, and when we returned to Iceland we got married and moved to the city. Thorsteinn worked for his father importing goods from America: vacuum cleaners especially. We had a nice house; Gudni was born. Times were hard before the war in Reykjavík, but Thorsteinn and his father were good businessmen.'

'Did you like Reykjavík?'

'Oh, yes. I go back there when I can. I stay with my aunt, and I often see my sister-in-law – Thorsteinn's sister – and her husband. And I get my hair done.'

Tom glanced at her red curls under her rather odd-looking hat. It was woollen with ear flaps and an intricate knitted pattern.

She smiled. 'You like my hat, don't you?'

'Very fashionable.'

'All the ladies in Hvalfjördur wear them. They are very warm. And you need a warm hat to ride an iron stallion.'

'You do indeed. So, your brother is in Copenhagen? Under the Germans? What's that like?'

'He's trying to get back to Iceland. It's very difficult, as you can imagine, but in his last letter he said that he and a group of Icelanders are planning to travel through Sweden to Finland.'

'Finland? Isn't that the wrong direction?'

'Apparently they can't cross the North Sea in case they are attacked and sunk, so they are planning to sail home from the north coast of Finland.'

'I didn't know Finland had a north coast.'

'Well, I hope it does. I'm worried about him.'

'Good luck to him,' said Tom. 'Your other brother doesn't like me much, does he?'

'Oh, don't worry about Siggi. He's just concerned about *Ástandid*.'

'*Ástandid*?' Tom looked the word up in his dictionary. '"The situation". What's that?'

'It's what they call "the Situation" that there are twenty thousand unattached young Englishmen and Canadians in Iceland and a much smaller number of unattached young women.'

'Oh, so the Icelandic men are worried that we'll steal all their women?'

'Don't laugh. I've heard that in Reykjavík they've started publishing in the newspaper the names of girls who go to dances with British soldiers.' She shuddered. 'And

God help any women who get pregnant. It's a bit early for that yet, but it's going to happen. Bound to.'

'Is your father concerned?' Tom asked. 'I hope not. I like your father.'

'And he likes you. You entertain him. And me.' She smiled.

Then she frowned. 'It was my fault. I told him and Siggi about something that happened in Reykjavík. It was actually the day the British landed.'

'Did someone bother you?'

'You could say that. I went to the bar of the Hótel Borg with my sister-in-law and her husband. Just to see what was going on. There was a rather attractive British officer there. I must have looked at him too long or something. I suppose I wouldn't have minded if he had come over to talk to us, but he didn't. Then we went home, and suddenly, when I was nearly at my aunt's house, he appeared out of nowhere.

'He started talking to me. At first, I told him I didn't understand, and then I told him to go away. In Icelandic, of course. He ignored it. I realized he was drunk. He held on to my arm.'

That angered Tom. British soldiers had been given stern lectures about not bothering the local women. And this man was an officer! 'Did he try to kiss you or anything?'

'He didn't get the chance. A soldier with three stripes on his shoulder came up and started talking to him. He told me to go home.' She laughed. 'And he gave the officer such a look. Like he was scum.' Tom had to quickly look that word up.

'Well, I apologize on behalf of my brother officer.' Tom meant it: he was ashamed. 'So Siggi thinks I might do the same as him?'

'What, get drunk and try to kiss me? I don't know what Siggi thinks.'

Tom didn't think the kissing bit of Siggi's idea was a bad one but decided not to say so.

'Have you ever been outside England?' Kristín asked. 'Apart from Iceland?'

'I've been to France and Switzerland. And I spent a summer with some cousins in Frankfurt when I was twenty. That's when I learned to speak German as well as read it.'

'Did you like the Germans?'

'I liked the family I stayed with and some of their friends. But they were Jewish. It was 1934, the Nazis had come to power and the persecution had started. Suddenly, ordinary Germans had permission to be beastly to Jews, and many were.'

'Are they still there, your cousins?'

'Yes. They believed it was all a passing fashion, that the Germans were too civilized to do real harm to the Jews. And by the time they realized things were not going to change, they couldn't leave the country. They're stuck there now.'

'Does that mean you're Jewish?' Kristín asked, her eyebrows raised.

'Yes,' said Tom. 'I'm not very religious, but I am Jewish. And I am proud to be Jewish.'

'I have never met a Jewish person before,' said Kristín. 'I don't think there are any in Iceland. There are some in Copenhagen, of course, but I didn't know any of them.'

'So what do you think? Of Jewish people?' Like all Jews in England, Tom had had to put up with occasional low-grade anti-Semitism his whole life. Nothing compared to Germany, of course, but if she didn't like him because of his religion, he wanted to know.

She smiled. 'I like the one I have met. So that is a one-hundred-per-cent success rate, isn't it?'

Tom liked that answer.

'Is that why you joined the army? Because of what the Germans were doing to the Jews?'

'Partly. I'm a schoolteacher. I got a job teaching after university, just because I didn't know what else to do. But actually, I like teaching small boys.'

'You are good with Gudni.'

'I realized that another war was coming. And yes, I wanted to fight the Germans. So I joined a territorial regiment. I was a part-time soldier until the war came. And now I'm a full-time soldier.'

'Defending Iceland.'

'I hope the Germans don't come. The generals seem to think they will, but I don't see how they can dodge the Royal Navy on the way here, or keep themselves supplied if they do land.'

Tom shook his head. 'It's ridiculous, really. We are fighting a great air battle over Britain to stop the Germans crossing the English Channel and we have twenty-five thousand men stuck up here a thousand miles away. Sometimes I wonder about our generals.'

'Generals are overrated. That's why we don't have any.'

'You borrow ours instead.'

'Not willingly.' Kristín sighed. 'I hope the Germans don't come. It would be strange to think of German soldiers marching here. Attacking Laxahóll.'

'I have to think about that all the time,' said Tom. 'That way, we will be ready. With our fourteen footballs – if you include Gudni's. Would he lend us his football, do you think?'

'I'm sure he would. Let's hope they haven't landed while you've been away,' said Kristín.

'Here, before we go. Let me take a photo of you.'

Tom pulled out his Brownie and took a picture of Kristín standing by the bike, her ridiculous hat on her head and Reykjavík in the distance behind.

NINE

September 2023

After dropping Vigdís off at police headquarters so she could drive her own car back to Hafnarfjördur, Magnus had gone straight off to Grafarholt to interview this Gudni.

It was such a shame about Audur. Vigdís had seemed pleased and proud that her mother had finally kicked the habit, although Magnus was aware of her underlying fear that that particular habit could never be kicked.

A fear that now seemed justified.

There were plenty of single mothers in Iceland, and the society was far more welcoming of the situation than many other countries, but most had a large Icelandic extended family to fall back on. Not Vigdís. Her black father had returned to America unaware of her existence. And her mother was useless. Worse than useless. Dangerous.

Yet Vigdís had known what she was getting herself into. She was an attractive woman, at least in Magnus's estimation: long legs, a lithe body, a certain aloofness that some men might find appealing rather than off-putting. She had had two serious boyfriends in the years Magnus had known her: an Icelandic TV executive based in New York and a German environmental activist. Both nice guys. Both in the wrong countries.

Magnus had assumed that Vigdís had resigned herself to no children, but then he had become aware that she was getting heavily involved in internet dating, of the one- or two-night-stand variety. When she had become pregnant – at the age of forty – Magnus had supposed she would be upset about it. Not a bit of it. She went through pregnancy with a serene smile of happiness.

Although Vigdís never acknowledged it publicly, Magnus had a pretty good idea who the father was.

The birth had been problem-free despite Vigdís's age, and there was no doubt that Erla had made her happy, even taking into account the occasional administrative hiccup.

As Magnus's own son Ási had made Ingileif happy.

Ingileif had been a bit younger than Vigdís when she had given birth – thirty-six rather than forty-one – but like Vigdís she had been careful not to acknowledge the father, or even tell him. Magnus had only found out when he and Vigdís had bumped into Ingileif and her four-year-old son in the street. And it was Vigdís who had spotted the similarity.

Now they were together, the three of them: Magnus, Ingileif and Ási, and all was well in Magnus's world.

But then, last weekend, Ingileif had done what Ingileif loved to do. Upset everything.

This time, it wasn't mischief-making. Quite the opposite. But for reasons Magnus didn't yet understand, it had had the same effect.

It was Sunday morning and they had been lying in bed

after a particularly vigorous and very satisfying half-hour of intense physical activity.

His breathing was just settling down. He reached over and stroked Ingileif's naked thigh gently. She purred.

He and Ingileif were right together. He had realized that very soon after they had first met, and it was a realization which had refused to go away during the ups and downs in their relationship since then.

In the long years when she had moved to Germany and then been married to someone else, there had been a few other women in Magnus's life, but he had never been able to summon up much enthusiasm for them. With the exception of the last, Eygló.

Yet even then, Ingileif had come back, and here he was.

Happy.

She raised herself up on her elbows and ran her finger down his cheek. She was smiling; her eyes were smiling. He noticed, as he always did at moments like this, that little V-shaped nick above her eyebrow, which had become so familiar over the years.

'So where shall we have it?'

'Have what?'

'The wedding.'

'What wedding?' Magnus was still stroking her thigh.

'Our wedding?'

Magnus's hand froze. 'Our wedding!'

'Yes. I've waited so long: I'd like a proper wedding. In a church. Perhaps that cute one at your grandparents' farm at Bjarnarhöfn?'

'What?'

'You know we're getting married, right? We agreed that when we got back together. I said we would have to be committed to each other. No sleeping around. And marriage. Didn't I say that?'

'You did. And we haven't slept around. Or at least I haven't.'

'And you think I have?'

'No, no! I know you haven't,' Magnus said. He couldn't trust Ingileif in the years before Ási was born, but then Ingileif hadn't professed belief in monogamy then. Now she did.

'But we also said we'd get married.'

'Er . . . *You* said that. I didn't.'

'I'd noticed,' said Ingileif. 'And I was waiting. For a proposal. I know what an old-fashioned American you are.'

'I know. And I'm sorry.'

'What's the matter?' said Ingileif. 'Don't you *want* to get married? I thought that's exactly what you wanted?'

'So did I. And I do. I think.' Magnus was confused. He did want to get married, didn't he? Hadn't he spent most of the last fourteen years wanting to get married to Ingileif? And yet. 'Can't we stay the way we are?'

'You're *such* an Icelander after all,' said Ingileif. 'But I want to do this.'

'Why?' said Magnus.

'Committing myself to you was a big deal for me. I'd like to do it properly. In front of our friends and what's left of our families. Make a public promise.'

'I see.'

'Don't you?'

'Yes.'

'Well, then? What's the problem?'

'I don't know, Ingileif,' Magnus had said. 'I just don't know.'

But there was a problem. And Magnus had to figure out what it was.

TEN

Gudni lived in a tiny apartment in a modern block on the crest of the hill at Grafarholt. As he rang the bell and waited for a response, Magnus looked out over a terrific view of Reykjavík, of the bay and of Mount Esja on the other side of Kollafjördur, slim clouds skimming its elongated summit, which was dusted with a sprinkling of snow. At that moment, the sun was painting Esja in a warm golden glow, but of course that could, and probably would, change within the hour.

When Magnus was old, he wouldn't mind spending his last years watching Esja.

Magnus had done some calculations, and if Frída's story was accurate, Gudni must be in his late eighties or early nineties. He looked younger – old, but not ancient. He was balding with long strands of white hair hanging over his ears. His small blue eyes were set close together and peered out through round glasses. Although his legs were stiff and his steps tiny, his movements were quick as he fetched Magnus a cup of coffee.

He was clearly excited about an unexplained visit from the police. And not just the police, a detective.

The flat was a shrine to the English football club Tottenham Hotspur. Posters, photographs, even a framed white shirt bearing the number 10 and the name 'Hoddle'. Gudni took his coffee in a Spurs mug, although Magnus's was emblazoned *Ísland Euro 2016*.

'Arsenal supporter, are you?' Magnus asked. He didn't know much about English football, but he did know who Spurs' big London rival was.

'How did you guess?' said Gudni. He looked around the room. 'I know it's a bit over the top. Way over the top. When my wife was alive I was only allowed one team photo in the toilet. But, a couple of years after she died, I thought, why not?'

'I'm an American football guy myself,' said Magnus. 'The Patriots.'

'That game's a mystery to me,' said Gudni. Then his smile disappeared. 'Oh, I know what you're here for.' The excitement seemed to leave him and his brows knitted. 'It's my mother, isn't it?'

Magnus nodded.

'Have you found her body?'

'It's too early to say for sure, but we may have. We need to do some forensic analysis to be certain.'

Gudni closed his eyes. 'I knew this would happen one day. Where is she?'

'In a gully between Selvík and Laxahóll farms.'

'Gerdur's Hollow?'

Magnus nodded.

'That figures.'

'Why does that figure?' said Magnus.

'Oh, it's near the farm. A good place to hide a body, and there was a landslide there during the war, which could be why it stayed hidden for so many years. There's also all that superstitious crap about a witch being buried there. We never believed any of that, but they did at Selvík.'

'They certainly do.'

'Did you find Uncle Marteinn too?'

Magnus nodded.

'You've spoken to Frída and her son?'

'We have. Jón was still freaked out by the story. Frída less so.'

'Yeah. Frída had a lot of common sense.'

'I suspect she still does. But the disappearance happened before she was born and she was unclear about the details. Can you fill me in?'

'I can try,' said Gudni. 'It happened in 1940. I was only six at the time. I can remember it very well, of course, it's one of my most abiding early memories, but I don't know the details of what went on.'

'Tell me what you do know.'

'I was in bed. There were three other people living in the house at that time: my mother Kristín, her brother Marteinn and my grandfather Hálfdán. Grandpa was out that day; I think he had been to Akranes. So it was just Mum and Uncle Marteinn. Grandpa came home late that evening and they weren't there.'

'No note or anything as to where they had gone?'

'Nothing. Grandpa woke me up when he got home, but I hadn't heard anything. I went back to sleep, but when I got up the next morning, they still hadn't shown up and Grandpa was in a right state. He dropped me off at Selvík and organized search parties. They didn't find them. I think he got the British involved – there was a camp fairly close and then the big naval base further up the fjord. But once again, nothing.'

'Why didn't they find the bodies if they were just in Gerdur's Hollow?'

Gudni shrugged. 'Maybe they were well hidden?' He knitted his brow. 'Thinking about it, it was probably the farmer at Selvík who was responsible for searching his own land. That would have been Frída's father, and he was the most superstitious of the lot of them.'

'So he may not have searched the hollow thoroughly?'

'It's just a guess. Is there any sign how they died? Were they caught by a landslide? Or was it something else?'

Magnus paused. 'They were shot,' he said. 'We found a bullet hole in one of the skulls. We assume the other victim was shot as well.'

That hit home as Magnus had feared it might. Gudni crumpled, and suddenly looked every one of his ninety or so years. A tear emerged in one eye. 'I'm sorry,' he said. Then more tears came and he began to sob.

Magnus hesitated and then got up to place a hand on the old man's arm.

Gudni smiled. 'I don't know why I'm doing this. I thought I had given up crying over Mum years ago.'

Back in Boston, Magnus had broken the bad news of the murder of a loved one to dozens of relatives over the years. That wasn't the worst part. The worst part was that the breaking of bad news was usually immediately followed up by intrusive questioning about the victim and their secrets.

It never got easier. Each relative was different, each suffering special. No matter how many times Magnus saw it, he never got used to it; it was what spurred him on to bring the victims' murderers to justice.

He sat back in the sofa and waited.

After a minute, Gudni wiped his nose and exhaled. 'Huh. It's probably best I got that out of my system. Do you have any more questions?'

'Yes. There was another brother, wasn't there? He would have been your uncle. Where was he?'

'Oh, yes. Uncle Siggi. He was working at the naval base at Hvammsvík, further up the fjord, so he wasn't home when it happened. But he came back to help with the search.'

'Now that you know your mother and your uncle were murdered, do you have any idea who might have done it? Were there any theories in the family that you can remember?'

'No. Uncle Siggi thought the British were involved somehow. The farmer at Selvík blamed it on Gerdur, which is ironic given he obviously didn't search her hollow very thoroughly. And Grandpa was just destroyed. He said he didn't understand it. His wife had died a couple of years earlier, as had my dad, who I scarcely remember. This was the final straw. He never recovered.'

'And what happened to you?' said Magnus.

'Grandpa looked after me, with Uncle Siggi. Siggi got married to Sunna from a farm near Akranes, who was really nice to me. Then Siggi ran off with Frída from Selvík and he got kicked out by Grandpa. Sunna stayed on with us until Grandpa sold the farm – in about 1970, I think. But by that stage, I was out of the house.'

'I assume none of these people are still alive?'

Gudni shook his dead. 'Just me. And Frída, but she wasn't born until the end of the war.'

Magnus scribbled some notes.

'If the bodies are theirs,' Gudni said, 'and if they were murdered, what will happen?'

'The district medical officer will prepare a death certificate and give it to the sheriff. And then there will be a funeral. You're the next of kin, so you'll get a copy of the certificate.'

'But no murder investigation?'

Magnus shook his head. 'Not eighty years later, when the murderer – whoever he was – is long dead. But can I take a DNA sample from you? That will be the best way to confirm that the body is your mother.'

Gudni nodded. Magnus had a kit with him. If there was a chance that the sample could be used in a trial, he would have had the swab taken at the station, but for the district medical officer and the sheriff, one taken by him in Gudni's flat would be fine.

As Gudni let Magnus out of his apartment, he paused. 'If you do figure out who killed her, you will let me know, won't you?'

After the detective had gone, Gudni shuffled quickly back to his favourite armchair and collapsed into it.

He stared across the room at the bookshelf against the far wall. And the old photograph album on its bottom shelf.

He levered himself up out of his chair and fetched it.

It was years since he had opened it. It always brought back a bittersweet mixture of memories. Happiness. Sadness. And horror.

It was the horror that kept him away from that album. But there was no hiding from that horror now.

He flipped through the pages. It was his mother's and it was only half full. He didn't think she had ever owned a camera, so the pictures must have been taken by her husband – Gudni's father – Grandpa and Tom. A couple at the end had certainly been taken by Tom.

He started at the beginning. The earliest of Mum was when she was aged about sixteen, taken outside Laxahóll. Tall, a little gawky, but beautiful. There were pictures of small brothers – Marteinn and Siggi – and then a dark handsome man appeared. Gudni's dad.

There were pictures of the wedding at the church at Laxahóll. Then of a house in Baldursgata in Reykjavík, with concrete steps leading up to the front door. Then of a baby and a toddler, a little Gudni.

Gudni leafed through to the end and his favourite two photographs: a young man in British Army uniform kicking a football to a six-year-old boy, and finally his mother standing by a motorcycle, the waters of Kollafjördur behind her, with the most gorgeous smile.

Gudni knew that the smile was directed at the man taking the picture, but he had always felt it was directed at him too, her son, from beyond the grave.

The grave that had now been found.

He closed the album. He smiled.

And then they came.

Those images that he knew would come. Of his mother. Of his uncle. Of those two pistol shots. Of the blood.

It wasn't the news that his mother had been shot which had hit him so hard.

It wasn't news. It was a memory that he had lived with for eighty years. And the policeman had brought it all back.

He closed his eyes and let out an animal howl.

Then he pulled out his phone and dialled a number.

'Dad?'

He tried to speak but he couldn't. He was aware of a whimper.

'Dad? Are you OK?'

'Something's happened, Bjarni. Can you come round, please? Now. Come now.'

ELEVEN

October 1940

'You've been rumbled, Tom.'

'What do you mean, sir?'

Tom was in Major Harris's office at Hvammsvík. The major tossed Tom a sheet of paper.

It was an order to Lieutenant Marks telling him to report to Captain Pybus-Smith at Divisional HQ at Ártún to assist with the interrogation of passengers expected to arrive in Reykjavík aboard the SS *Esja* from Petsamo in Finland.

'Why me, sir?'

'As I said, they've rumbled you. They know you speak Icelandic.'

'Hardly, sir. I'm certainly not good enough to interpret.'

'I told HQ that, but they still want you. The good news is that you'll be put up at the Hotel Borg. A couple of days in Reykjavík won't do you any harm, eh?'

'Do you know this Pybus-Smith, sir?'

'I've met him a couple of times. He's military intelligence. He's frightfully keen – believes there is a spy under every Icelandic bed. To be fair to him, they've caught two already. He seems a decent fellow, but . . .'

'Sir?'

'I don't altogether trust him.'

Tom rode the Enfield to divisional headquarters, a few miles before Reykjavík. It took him half an hour to learn that the captain was expecting Tom at a warehouse by the harbour in Reykjavík.

Reykjavík was bustling, especially in the harbour area. British merchant ships were backed up from the docks. The air was alive with clanks, crashes, shouts and the grinding of engines as cranes strained and forklifts buzzed around wharves crammed with crates, vehicles and munitions.

A section of Canadian Cameron Highlanders marched past, bayonets fixed, kilts swirling, stared at by a group of small blond Icelandic boys. One of the urchins lifted his arm in a swift *Heil Hitler* salute and ran, followed by his laughing comrades. A Canadian corporal broke step to give chase, but then thought better of it.

Just a short distance away, Icelandic fishing boats brushed up against another quay, and a row of burly women were filleting that day's catch on long tables, their arms and aprons smeared in blood and guts. The smell of fish pervaded the air.

Tom found the warehouse, and Captain Pybus-Smith. He was a tall, dapper man with a thin moustache. He held himself like a gentleman, rather than an officer, and Tom guessed he wasn't regular army. He greeted Tom with an affable smile, a pipe sticking out of the corner of his mouth.

'Good of you to come, Marks,' he said. 'That's the *Esja* there.' He pointed to a small passenger ship with a single funnel, tied up to the quayside.

'The passengers are all Icelanders returning from Copenhagen. Many of them were students studying there: some of them are the sons of bigwigs in Iceland.' He chuckled. 'If there is such a thing as an Icelandic bigwig, what?'

Tom smiled politely.

'Anyway, they made their way from Copenhagen to Finland and a port on the Barents Sea called Petsamo, where the *Esja* met them. They steamed from there to Scapa Flow where they have been screened. But I think we should screen them again, just to be on the safe side.'

'Screen them for what, sir? Spying?'

'That's the idea. It would be a piece of cake for Jerry to smuggle one of their agents on board, or, better yet, turn one of the Icelanders to their cause. So, we're looking for Nazis. And communists.'

'Communists?'

'After the Nazi–Soviet Pact last year, we need to beware of communists. A rum lot at the best of times, but it's just possible the Nazis might recruit a Bolshie against us, you know?'

'I see. What would you like me to do, sir? I speak a little Icelandic, but nowhere near enough to be a reliable interpreter.'

'I have a good interpreter, Gunnar Árnason. He's only nineteen, but he's trustworthy. At least, I *think* he is. What I'd like you to do is sit in on the first interviews. Listen to the translation and tell me afterwards whether it's accurate or whether there's any funny stuff going on. Then perhaps, once you've seen how it's done, we can split up and tackle the rest separately.'

'Will the interpreter know that I speak some Icelandic?'

Pybus-Smith chuckled. 'No. And I'd rather he didn't.'

'I see, sir. Won't he find out at some point? Isn't there a risk you'll lose his trust?'

'Oh, Gunnar knows me and my little schemes well. He won't be surprised. Let's get cracking, shall we?'

There were 250 passengers on the *Esja*, many of them male students from Iceland's wealthier families, but also a hundred women and twenty-three children. They were let off the boat in small groups while they were 'screened', some of them pulled to one side for Pybus-Smith to question more closely. He asked these passengers – all men – about their family in Iceland, their political beliefs and affiliations, whether they had travelled outside Denmark – and he always threw a question in German at them to see whether they spoke the language.

The passengers were tired, bemused and nervous. Some of the older ones were offended, but this didn't go down well with Pybus-Smith.

From what Tom could tell, Gunnar the young translator was doing a very good job.

Tom was on the lookout for a Marteinn Hálfdánsson and, sure enough, he was eventually ushered into the simple interview room, which was nothing more than a small concrete storage shed with a desk and four chairs.

He looked a little like Kristín and a lot like Hálfdán. Like Hálfdán and Siggi, but unlike his sister, he was short. He had reddish hair and an impish smile, which failed to impress Pybus-Smith. Neither did his answers.

Tom could tell that the fact that he came from a farm in Hvalfjördur raised the captain's suspicions, as did Marteinn's admission that his brother was working on the construction of the naval base there. But it was his membership of the Communist Party that really worried Pybus-Smith.

'When did you become a member?' he asked, the young interpreter translating.

'About six months ago,' said Marteinn. 'While I was in Copenhagen. That was one of the reasons I went there, to study Marxism.'

'Are your family communists?'

Marteinn snorted. 'My father is a member of the Independence Party and always will be.'

'And your brother? The one who works at the base?'

'He's only eighteen. He was seventeen last time I saw him, and he had no interest in politics.'

'So, you are sympathetic to socialism. What about National Socialism?'

'I'm no Nazi. The Nazis invaded Denmark. I have seen the Nazis at close quarters and I don't like them.'

'But the Soviet Union is allied to Germany?'

'Not exactly allied.'

'They made a pact to carve up Poland.'

'They did,' Marteinn admitted. 'And I don't know why. I don't understand why the Soviet Union doesn't oppose Hitler. It must have its reasons.'

'And what do you think about the British presence in Iceland?'

Marteinn considered his answer. He chose honesty. 'The British were uninvited. It was an invasion, an occupation.'

'Like the Nazi occupation of Denmark?'

'Not quite that bad, but yes.'

Pybus-Smith puffed at his pipe. 'Would you prefer it if the British left?'

'Yes,' said Marteinn simply.

Part of Tom admired Marteinn's honesty. Part of him wished he would just lie.

Pybus-Smith turned to Tom. 'What do you think?' he asked in a voice low enough so that even if Marteinn understood English, he wouldn't hear.

'I know his family,' Tom said. 'Their farm isn't far from my platoon in Hvalfjördur.'

'Really?' Pybus-Smith raised his eyebrows. 'And?'

'His father, Hálfdán, is a good man and has always been perfectly civil to me. He welcomes the British being here – says we're better than the Germans.'

'I should bally well hope so. And the younger brother? The one who works at the base. What's he like?'

'A sullen blighter,' Tom said.

'Does he like the British?'

Tom was tempted to lie, but he was a British officer doing his duty. 'No. He's worried we'll take his women.'

Pybus-Smith grinned. 'Oh, that! So, what do you think? About Hálfdánsson?'

'I think he's all right,' Tom said. 'I know you said we should be suspicious of communists, but I think his only fault is he answered your questions honestly. He may not like us being here, but there's no indication that he would help the Germans.'

'I'm not so sure,' said Pybus-Smith. 'Let's keep him overnight. Talk to him again tomorrow. Next!'

TWELVE

They took a break and went outside for some fresh air. Pybus-Smith lit his pipe, and Tom a cigarette.

'So how is Gunnar?' Pybus-Smith asked.

'From what I can tell, his translations are faithful. I'm impressed.'

Pybus-Smith smiled. 'Excellent. He's a good man; I thought I could trust him. I'm glad to have it confirmed.' He drew on his pipe, cupping it in his hand to protect it from the persistent breeze.

'They're basically a good lot, the Icelanders,' he said. 'I'm not sure how I would feel if a bunch of foreigners showed up in my capital city, even if they had the best of intentions. So, I'm not surprised there are some bad apples who would rather we were gone. Doesn't excuse it, though, especially if they are hoping for Jerry to get rid of us.'

They smoked in silence for a moment, watching the women attacking the fish on the quayside. It looked hard work.

'Sir?'

'Yes?'

'It's difficult to rely on what the passengers are telling us about themselves, isn't it? I mean, we ask them questions, but if any of them really were German spies they would just lie to us, wouldn't they?'

'They'd try,' said Pybus-Smith. 'We might rumble them anyhow. But I take your point.'

'What if we asked them about the other passengers on the ship? They must know each other very well by now, having travelled for a month together. They probably knew each other anyway in Copenhagen or back in Iceland. We could ask if there are any Nazi sympathizers on the boat. Or members of the Icelandic Nazi party.'

'Or communists?'

'Or communists,' Tom conceded.

'They could still lie to us. Cover for their friends.'

'If they were friends. But they've all been under German rule in Denmark. They're glad to be here not there. I'm sure some of them would be happy to tell us about any Nazis if we asked in the right way.' By 'in the right way' Tom meant nicely.

'I see what you mean,' said Pybus-Smith, puffing at his pipe. 'Good idea. Let's try it. And we've still got a lot of passengers to go, so you take interviews by yourself from now on.'

'Yes, sir.' Given the state of Tom's Icelandic, the interviews might be a little stilted, but he would cope.

'By the way, I managed to get you into the Hotel Borg tonight.'

'I know, sir, thank you.'

'Shall we have a drink in the bar when we've finished here? I'd like to chat to you about a little matter.'

'Right you are, sir.' He wondered what the 'little matter' was. He could guess, but he hoped he was wrong.

Neville sauntered off, and Tom finished his cigarette. The sun had put in a brief ten-minute appearance, and Tom wanted to enjoy it.

'*Góđan daginn.*'

Tom recognized the voice and turned to see Kristín smiling at him, dressed in a smart skirt and jacket, her hair nicely curled under a stylish green hat.

'What are you doing here?' he asked.

'I'm here to meet Marteinn. He was on board that ship.'

'I know,' said Tom, sheepishly.

'You know?'

'Yes, I interviewed him. I'm afraid he won't be ready to leave today. We are keeping him overnight.'

Kristín frowned. 'Keeping him overnight? Why?'

'We think he might be a spy.'

Kristín opened her mouth in horror. 'For the Germans! That's ridiculous. Why?'

'Because he's a communist.'

'He's not a communist. A socialist, maybe, but not a communist.'

'He told us he'd joined the party in Denmark.'

'Really? Anyway, so what? That doesn't mean he's a German spy, does it? You must be crazy, Tom.'

'I know it doesn't,' said Tom. 'But Captain Pybus-Smith thinks communists are suspicious.'

'And couldn't you tell him he's an idiot?'

Tom smiled. 'I couldn't. I did say I knew Marteinn's family and that your father was very civil to me. I recommended we release him.'

Kristín controlled her anger. 'I'm sure you did. Is this captain the man you were talking to just now? With the thin moustache and walrus teeth?'

Tom grinned at the description. 'That's him.'

'Hm. Well, you had better let my brother go tomorrow morning.'

'I'll try.' If Tom had thought for a moment that Marteinn was a Nazi spy, he would have been more circumspect. But it was clear he wasn't. He was just honest, that was his problem.

'Look, I'm staying at the Hótel Borg. Do you want to join me for a drink later?'

'Will that captain be there?'

'Yes,' said Tom. 'But that may be a chance for you to talk him round, as a member of Marteinn's family. I'll translate. With Ari the Learned's help.' He waved his faithful dictionary.

'Maybe,' said Kristín doubtfully. 'I'll think about it.'

With that, she was gone, and Tom returned to the storage shed and more interviews.

Tom's plan worked nicely. Everyone knew that three of the passengers on the *Esja* were Nazi sympathizers – one was actually a member of the tiny Icelandic Nationalist Party. There were also four possible communists, one of whom was Marteinn, although no one Tom spoke to thought that Marteinn could possibly be a German spy.

Tom discussed his results with Pybus-Smith, who had come to a similar conclusion. He wanted to keep the seven suspects overnight, including Marteinn, to interrogate them tomorrow, despite Tom's suggestion that they let the communists go.

It turned out that Pybus-Smith did have some reason to be concerned about the communists. *Thjódviljinn*, a left-wing newspaper which meant *The Will of the Nation*, had been agitating against the British, blaming them for the potato shortage and claiming that a British soldier had had sex with a fourteen-year-old girl and given her a venereal disease. Pybus-Smith thought the newspaper was funded by Moscow. It only had a circulation of about fifteen hundred, but he was worried about it nonetheless.

Of course, that didn't mean Marteinn was a spy for the Nazis.

'I do like this place,' said Neville as he bought Tom a whisky and soda at the bar of the Borg. 'I managed to get myself billeted here when we arrived. Got turfed out eventually, though. It's easily the best place in Reykjavík.'

'It certainly beats Hvalfjördur,' Tom said.

Pybus-Smith lit his pipe, raising his eyes at Tom inquiringly. 'Marks a Jewish name, isn't it?'

Here we go, thought Tom. 'It is.'

'Where are your family from?'

'London. Hampstead.'

'I mean originally?'

'The East End, I believe.' Tom was an Englishman and wasn't going to let Pybus-Smith imply otherwise.

'Hampstead, eh?' Pybus-Smith puffed at his pipe. 'Are you a bit of a Bolshie yourself?'

'I beg your pardon?'

'I was just wondering. All those left-wing intellectuals in Hampstead. Your reaction to that communist.'

'Whom I vote for is my own business.'

'Not if you're in intelligence, it's not.'

'But I'm not in intelligence.'

'Not yet,' said Pybus-Smith with a smile. 'You mustn't mind my awkward questions, old man. You did a good job today. We work well together, and I could use a British officer who speaks Icelandic.' He grinned. 'Surely you'd rather be stationed here than on the shore of some godforsaken fjord?'

So that was what the 'little matter' was. Tom wasn't surprised. He wasn't at all sure he wanted to work with Pybus-Smith but he realized it would make everyone's life easier if he denied being a communist.

'I voted for the National Government in the last election.'

'Good man.'

Pybus-Smith stiffened as he saw something over Tom's shoulder. Then he reddened and swivelled towards the bar.

Tom turned to see Kristín approaching him, smiling. Everyone else in the bar was turning towards her rather than away from her.

'Good evening, Tom,' she said.

'Hello,' said Tom. 'I'm glad you came. Can I get you a drink?'

'I can't stay long,' she said. 'But, yes, I would like one. Can I have a gin and vermouth?'

Ari the Learned wasn't really up to that one, but Kristín explained it to the barman.

'Oh, let me introduce you to Captain Pybus-Smith. This is Kristín Hálfdánsdóttir.'

'We have met,' said Kristín, smiling at the captain, who was looking excruciatingly embarrassed.

Tom raised his eyebrows and translated.

'Have we?' said Pybus-Smith.

'Oh, yes. You were a little drunk.'

'Was I?' Pybus-Smith frowned as if trying to remember, but he was obfuscating. 'Oh, yes, yes. Yes, I do remember.'

'Well?' said Kristín, raising her eyebrows.

It took Pybus-Smith a few moments to realize what she

was waiting for. 'Um. I'm sorry. I'm afraid I might have made a bit of an ass of myself.'

Tom frantically translated this, choosing the Icelandic word for 'horse' for 'ass' in his haste.

'You did,' Kristín said, with a hint of a smile at Tom's translation. 'You were quite a horse.'

'I apologize. I hope there was no harm done?'

Kristín gave Pybus-Smith a dazzling smile. 'No, none whatsoever. Men get drunk in Iceland all the time. I'm used to it.'

So it was Pybus-Smith who had propositioned Kristín the night of the occupation! Tom's amazement turned to anger. The cad!

Pybus-Smith and Kristín were both looking at him, waiting for him to translate. Tom decided that firstly, he would not give Pybus-Smith any sign that Kristín had told him about that evening, and secondly, if Kristín wanted to forgive Pybus-Smith, presumably so that he would release her brother, that was her business.

She came straight to the point. She tended to do that.

'I came to Reykjavík to pick up my brother, but Tom tells me you suspect him of being a German spy?'

'We can't be too careful,' said Pybus-Smith, nodding his head solemnly. 'And he admits he is a communist.'

'But he *hates* the Nazis,' said Kristín. 'Which means he hates the Germans. I can assure you the last thing Marteinn would ever do is help them.'

'Ah,' said Pybus-Smith. 'That's good to know. Thank you for telling me.'

Kristín gave him another dazzling smile. 'This is Iceland. I can't call you Captain Pybus-Smith. What is your real name?'

Pybus-Smith smiled nervously. 'Neville.'

'Well, Neville. How do you like Iceland?'

They spoke for fifteen minutes, Kristín charming Pybus-Smith in her rather blunt, direct way, Tom translating furiously with the occasional help of Ari the Learned.

Tom understood what Kristín was doing, but he didn't like it. If Marteinn wasn't a spy, he would be released soon anyway. Pybus-Smith didn't deserve to be absolved from what was seriously ungentlemanly behaviour.

Also, he was unimpressed with Kristín being so charming to another man.

A tall, fair-haired Icelander in a double-breasted suit entered the bar and approached her.

'Ah, Sigursteinn! This is my brother-in-law, Sigursteinn,' Kristín said to Tom and Pybus-Smith.

The two British officers smiled and shook the Icelander's hand. There was not a crack of a smile back.

'Sigursteinn has come to escort me back to my aunt's house,' said Kristín. 'Goodbye, Neville. It was very nice to talk to you properly.'

Tom was glad to see she had taken that precaution this time. He suspected Sigursteinn knew all about Pybus-Smith.

'Come and visit us at Laxahóll, Neville,' she said. 'Tom will tell you where we are. We are always welcoming, aren't we, Tom?'

Before translating, Tom replied to her in Icelandic. 'Are you crazy?'

'I'll be perfectly safe,' said Kristín. 'He will sit with me and Dad and drink coffee and eat cakes for fifteen minutes and then he will go. He doesn't speak Icelandic and we don't speak English. Just translate it.'

'All right,' said Tom, and he did as he was asked.

'That's jolly kind,' said Pybus-Smith, with a grin that

was almost as charming as Kristín's. 'I may well take you up on that.'

Tom and Pybus-Smith watched Kristín leave the bar with her unsmiling escort.

'Quite a girl, that one. She was jolly decent about the last time we met. I did make an ass of myself with her, I'm ashamed to say. She seems to have quite forgiven me, don't you think?'

'She does,' Tom admitted grudgingly.

'And she vouched for Hálfdánsson. Said he hated the Germans.'

'That's true.'

'I think we'll let him go in the morning, don't you, Marks?'

Much later, Tom was tucked up in his bedroom at the Hotel Borg, reading a Graham Greene 'entertainment', when he heard a gentle knock at the door.

He hopped out of bed and opened it.

Kristín.

She smiled nervously.

'I have come to discuss "the Situation" with you. If that's all right?'

'That's quite all right,' said Tom with a broad smile. 'Come in.'

THIRTEEN

September 2023

Erla was better the next morning, so Vigdís was able to take her into day care. She called Magnus to ask him if she could be late for work because she had to check on her mother.

She was furious. Absolutely furious. But she was also worried.

Her mother should be at work – at the Bónus supermarket on the outskirts of Keflavík – and, somewhat to Vigdís's surprise, she was.

She looked haggard at the checkout, but Vigdís was pleased that she hadn't just gone home and started on a multi-day bender.

Audur reddened with shame when she saw Vigdís. 'I'm on a break in ten minutes,' she said. 'Can we talk then?'

Vigdís met her at the back of the supermarket. Two other employees were puffing greedily at cigarettes, but Vigdís took her mother by the arm so they were safely out of earshot.

'How could you do that, Mum?'

Audur looked at her daughter with red-rimmed, watery eyes. 'I'm sorry.'

'You completely abused my trust in you. Something could have happened to Erla. And then you almost killed a jogger!'

'You know about that?'

'I saw it! Through the window. And I called you a cab. I *told* you to take a cab. Why didn't you? You were drunk and you hit that guy. And then you drove off. What were you thinking? Why didn't you just do what I asked you to do?'

'I wasn't thinking. I was angry with you.'

'Why?'

'Because you were being so bossy.'

'Someone had to be bossy! Someone had to tell you what to do!'

Audur winced. 'I know, Vigdís, I know. It's not because you were wrong. It's because you were right. I've let you down and Erla down.'

'But why, Mum? Why? You were doing so well. Or I thought you were doing well. When did it start?'

'I had a drink last month. I was in a bar here in Keflavík with a woman from work. She didn't know my history. She bought me a drink and I was confident I could just have the one. It was a glass of white wine. It tasted good, and I stuck at one. No problem.

'And then I did it again, two weeks ago. One drink, no problem.'

'And yesterday? You drank almost a whole bottle of gin?'

Audur glanced at Vigdís nervously. 'I was in such a good mood that you had let me take care of Erla. She went down for a nap. I saw the bottle of gin. I thought, one little drink to celebrate. I know I can handle one drink.'

She sighed. 'So I had the one drink and the gin tasted really good – better than the wine had done. Erla carried on napping. I thought if I can have one drink, I can have two.' Audur raised her hands in a gesture of helplessness. 'What about the guy I hit?'

'Oh, he's OK. I was worried at first – he was knocked unconscious, and it looked like he had a broken rib – and they took him to hospital. I called the hospital last night. They said the rib was just bruised and the man was fine. Because there was a head injury, they were keeping him in overnight, but he's probably out by now.'

'You said you saw me hit him. Did you report it?'

'No,' said Vigdís. Her mother smiled. Vigdís didn't. 'Not yet.'

'Are you going to?'

'I don't know. I don't know what I'm going to do with you, Mum. I can't let you see Erla when you're drunk. And I can't ever let you be alone with her.'

A tear appeared in Audur's eye. 'Look, Vigdís. I know I screwed up, but I've done really well these last couple of years. And it was all because of Erla; I know I have to stay clean if I'm going to be a proper grandmother for her. I'll keep going to AA meetings. If you like, I'll go back to rehab. I just got overconfident and stupid. I think I can catch it now. If you help me.'

'But you've said that so many times before!'

'Not like this,' said Audur. 'I mean it. You know I mean it! For Erla's sake.'

Vigdís watched her mother. She believed she did mean it. And it was true that in past years when she fell off the wagon she had fallen right off it and stayed off it. This time felt different.

'You know, if you tell them you saw me hit that guy and drive off, they'll send me to prison again,' Audur said.

'I know, Mum. And you'd deserve it.' Audur had spent a couple of months in prison several years before for assaulting a boyfriend while drunk. So she had a record.

'Maybe I do deserve it. But if I go to prison, then I'm damned sure I won't pull myself together.'

'Are you threatening me?' Vigdís said, anger rising once more. 'What – if I report you, you'll get drunk again?'

'No, love,' said Audur sadly. 'It's not a threat. It's just what will happen. You do what you have to do.'

FOURTEEN

'Do you have a firm ID of the victims, Magnús?'

Detective Superintendent Thelma Reynisdóttir latched her blue no-bullshit eyes on Magnus. She was a tough cop, but she trusted her detective inspector. Mostly. They had been working together long enough that they knew each other's strengths. And weaknesses.

'Pretty firm. They are probably Kristín Hálfdánsdóttir and her brother Marteinn. They went missing on 28 October 1940 from the farm at Laxahóll which is only a kilometre away from where the bodies were discovered. I dug the old case file out. There was a major search, but no theory as to why they disappeared or whether they had been killed – some locals blamed the British, but with no real evidence. A shotgun was missing from the farm. A neighbour said he saw a large blue car driving up the road towards the farm, but the vehicle was never identified. The police got assistance from the British Army in the search and liaised with the British in the investigation, but they didn't come up with anything.'

Magnus checked his notes. 'One of the skulls had a

bullet hole in it, and we found a bullet with the other skeleton, so it's likely they were both shot. The bullet is a thirty-eight millimetre, of the kind that was used in an Enfield Number Two revolver. Those were standard issue for officers in the British Army at the time.'

'Interesting. Anything on the age of the bones?'

'The forensic pathologist won't say – the timing of skeletonization is tricky. I'm getting them radiocarbon-dated at the university; that should give us some idea. One is a tall young woman and one a shortish young man, which fits the brother and sister theory.'

'Any of the family still alive?'

'Just Kristín's son, Gudni. He was six when she went missing. He says that no one knew what had happened, although there were rumours the British Army may have had something to do with it. I took a sample of Gudni's DNA, which should confirm the bones belong to his close relatives.' Unfortunately, the DNA had to be sent to a lab in Sweden for analysis, which could take time.

Thelma nodded. 'So, assuming your ID is correct, we're looking at a murder in 1940, with no obvious suspects and no way of finding any?'

'I suppose that's right. It could have been a British officer, but then again an Icelander could have got hold of an Enfield revolver somehow during the war.'

'Whoever did kill them is dead by now, right? The six-year-old can't have done it.'

'Right.'

Thelma leaned back in her chair, and then gave Magnus one of her piercing stares.

'This case piques your curiosity, Magnús.'

Magnus nodded. 'It does.'

'Thought so. But this job isn't for your amusement. I

don't want you spending any more resources on it than are necessary. If the DNA analysis shows that the bodies are Gudni's relatives, then the case is closed. I suppose, if it doesn't, or if the carbon dating suggests the bones are newer, you should investigate further. But something bothers me.'

'Oh, yes?'

'If the press finds out it was probably a British bullet that killed these people, especially the woman, it might stir up all kinds of trouble. People will ask us who we think killed her. Then they'll ask the British, who will get defensive. The newspapers might dredge up "the Situation".' Thelma nodded to herself. 'This could waste an enormous amount of time.'

'I see what you mean,' said Magnus. 'But there will be a death certificate. And probably a funeral. Local people will know who the victims were and that they were murdered.'

'Yes, but the fewer details they have, the better. The less we know, the less we can tell them. And I don't think anyone needs to know about the bullet possibly being British, do you?'

'Not even the son?'

'Better if he doesn't, don't you think? And certainly don't tell the press. This can be either an interesting small story or a pain-in-the-arse big story. Let's make sure it's a small story, eh?'

To some extent, Magnus saw Thelma's point, although he wasn't convinced that anyone really would draw a link to 'the Situation'. And, whilst this was hardly a live murder investigation, it was a matter of legitimate historical interest. He wasn't sure the police should be hiding information from historians.

Arguing with Thelma was always a bad idea. And you

could say that solving this crime was a job for historians rather than policemen.

'I'll let you know when we hear back from Sweden on the DNA, and then I'll wrap the case up,' Magnus said.

Back at his desk, there was indeed a message from a reporter at *Morgunbladid.* Magnus called him back and confirmed that two bodies had been found which had been shot. At this stage, he wouldn't speculate on whose the bodies were, but it was likely they were at least two years old, probably much older.

Once *Morgunbladid* published the story online and in the newspaper tomorrow morning, there would be interest from the other news outlets: newspapers, news websites and TV. That would probably die down and then there would be another flurry of interest when the skeletons were carbon-dated and they received DNA ID confirmation from Sweden.

He had his instructions.

But Thelma was right, he *was* curious. How could he not be? Someone had murdered that brother and sister in cold blood, and likely as not it had been a British officer.

Magnus didn't know much about the British occupation of Iceland in the 1940s. He knew some 'spies' had been arrested, and there had been a couple of inadvertent shootings of Icelanders who strayed into camps at night by the Americans who took over from the British, but this sounded like murder.

Why would the British shoot two civilians?

Vigdís arrived. She looked upset, unsurprisingly.

'How's your mother?' Magnus asked.

'Better than I feared,' Vigdís said. 'She's sober and she's at work. I was afraid I would find her still drinking at home.'

'So she was drunk with Erla?'

Vigdís nodded.

'I'm sorry, Vigdís. I know you've tried so hard. But, at the end of the day, it's up to her, isn't it?'

Magnus's own mother had been an alcoholic. She had died in a car crash while drunk when he was twelve – that's why he and his brother had moved to America to be with their Icelandic father. That experience hadn't given him any insight into how to deal with alcoholics, but it had certainly taught him the pain it could bring to families.

Vigdís frowned. She looked around the room at the other police officers tapping at keyboards or staring at computer screens. 'Can we get a coffee? I need your advice.'

She led him to a small coffee shop a couple of hundred metres from the station. Cop free.

'I don't know what to do.'

'About what?'

'Mum hit a jogger. When she was driving home from my place.'

'What! Is he all right?'

'Yes. They kept him in hospital for observation, but he's fine.'

'And did she drive off?'

Vigdís nodded.

'Then how do you know? Did she tell you?' It clicked. 'She didn't tell you. But you saw it?'

Vigdís nodded.

'And you didn't report it?'

'Not yet. I didn't tell the cop who attended the scene.'

'Well, you should. If you do it now, you'll be OK. They'll be understanding. But you have to do it right away.'

'You remember Mum has a record? She'll probably go to jail again. And then I'll have lost her, for sure.'

'Whereas if she's still running around driving cars into people when she's drunk everything will be fine?'

'She won't be. She says she'll go to rehab. She says she's been clean for over a year. She says it's Erla who will keep her straight.'

'She says.' Magnus didn't hide his scepticism.

'Yes, she says. And I believe her. I not only believe her, I think it's her best chance.'

'She's pulling you down with her, Vigdís. That's what they do, alcoholics. If you don't report her you're breaking the rules. Hell, now you've told me, *I'm* breaking the rules. I now know a crime has been committed.'

Vigdís's eyes flashed. 'You're not going to report her, are you? Because that would be reporting me!'

'No, of course I'm not,' said Magnus. 'But you see what she's doing?'

Vigdís sipped her coffee. Her lips were pursed and she avoided Magnus's glance, staring at the salt cellar between them.

Magnus lowered his voice. 'You asked for my advice,' he said gently. 'It's this. Report what you saw and do it now. That's the right thing to do.'

Vigdís looked up, her brown eyes filled with doubt and pain.

'Yeah. I did ask. And I suppose I know you're right. But I'm not sure I can bring myself to do that to her.'

Magnus decided to leave it. He had made his point. He hoped he had persuaded her. 'Let's get back to work.'

FIFTEEN

Vigdís had gone home early, and Magnus was tidying up his desk ready to follow her when his phone pinged.

It was a text from his brother Ollie back in Boston: a photo of Tosci's Ice Cream in Cambridge – no comment. They had gone there as kids; Ollie, in particular, loved the place. Magnus could still taste the mint chocolate chip which had been his own go-to flavour.

Magnus selected a bland emoji – he wasn't very good at emojis – and replied.

Ollie had started sending him the odd joke or picture of places from their childhood. Thirteen years before, when Magnus had finally discovered that Ollie had been indirectly implicated in their father's murder, Ollie had gone to jail. He had been out for years now, but the brothers had barely spoken. Until Ollie had shown up in Iceland unannounced with a couple of buddies, just after one of the COVID lockdowns was lifted. The group was on their way to London, which had also just opened up, and had decided to travel via Iceland.

Magnus, Ollie and his two friends, Ryan and Cal,

together with Vigdís, had gone out for a traditional Friday night on the town in Reykjavík.

It was only the second time Ollie had been back to Iceland since he and Magnus had left as kids to join their father in Boston. Ollie claimed that when his friends had suggested that they stop off in the land of Ollie's birth, he had thought, why not?

Perhaps that was true. Or perhaps Ollie had welcomed the excuse to see his brother.

A lot of alcohol had been drunk; nothing of any consequence had been said. But Magnus enjoyed spending some time with his little brother having some fun.

It was about 1 a.m. and they were in a crowded bar off Laugavegur. Vigdís had gone to the bathroom – she was as drunk as the rest of them. Ollie's two buddies had found a pair of women who seemed to find their jokes amusing.

'Do you think they'll get lucky?' Ollie asked Magnus with a grin.

Magnus glanced at the foursome and nodded. 'I'm sure they'll get lucky. Unless they fall over before they get the chance.'

Ollie laughed. He took a gulp of his beer and nodded at Vigdís's empty chair. 'She's hot,' he said.

'She's a nice woman,' Magnus said primly. 'And a good friend.'

'She wants you so bad,' said Ollie.

Magnus snorted. 'No, she doesn't. We've been working together for years. We know each other too well for that.'

'Oh yes, she does,' said Ollie. 'I can tell. And if I were you, I'd let her.'

'You do talk shit,' Magnus said. But for a moment he wondered if Ollie had a point. Then he remembered it was always a mistake to wonder if Ollie had a point. 'I have a girlfriend, Ollie.'

'Everyone has a girlfriend. Or a wife. Ryan has a wife and Cal a long-term girlfriend. Doesn't matter. Especially here, from what I've read.'

'Slurs,' Magnus slurred.

'Says you.'

Ollie leaned over and tried to focus on his brother. 'Do you know at one point I was worth almost ten million dollars?'

'Crypto?'

'That's right.'

'I thought everyone had lost their shirt on that?'

'Not everyone. You gotta know when to get in and when to get out.'

'And you did?'

Ollie grinned and waggled his head. 'Not quite. But I'm still in the game. Just.'

'Well, thanks for the warning on Thomocoin.' Magnus had asked Ollie about the cryptocurrency the year before during an investigation in North Iceland and Ollie, quite curtly, had warned him off it.

'I was right,' said Ollie. 'Wasn't I? You know it blew up?

'I did know that,' said Magnus with a wry smile.

'You see? I keep my eyes out for you. Just like you did for me.'

Recalling that evening two years before, Magnus felt an unexpected swirl of sentiment towards his little brother.

For years, Magnus had looked after Ollie. Then he had rejected him – they had rejected each other. Ollie's partial involvement in the death of their father was unforgivable, as was, in Ollie's mind, Magnus testifying at his trial.

But there were just the two of them.

Perhaps anything was forgivable eventually.

If he and Ingileif did get married, would he invite Ollie to the wedding? Would Ollie come?

The more important question was: should he and Ingileif get married? He had to face up to that one.

His phone rang. It was the front desk: a British woman wanted to see him. She had given her name as Louisa Sugarman.

The Englishwoman whose email address Frída had given him.

Interesting.

A woman in her sixties with short, expensively cut blonde hair was waiting for him. Even though she was wearing the classic tourist garb of rain jacket and jeans, she had poise as she smiled, held out her hand and fixed him with an intelligent and authoritative gaze.

'Inspector Ragnarsson?' she said. 'You sent me an email yesterday saying you had found Kristín Hálfdánsdóttir's remains. I thought I'd reply in person.'

Magnus raised his eyebrows. 'Were you in Iceland? I assumed you were in England.'

'I was. But I jumped on a plane immediately.'

Magnus was intrigued. 'Well, let's get us some coffee and you can tell me why.'

He led her upstairs to his desk via the coffee machine. 'When did you arrive?' he asked her.

'Just a couple of hours ago. I dumped my suitcase at my Airbnb and came straight here. I wanted to get you before you went home.'

'What's the rush? The poor woman has been dead for eighty years. Why not just send me an email, or call?'

The woman sipped her coffee, examining Magnus with steady brown eyes.

'Kristín's death is important to me,' she said. 'I want to find answers. And I suspect that the best way to find them is to come here myself to get them.'

'That's probably true. But why is this woman so important to you? She must have died many years before you were born. Something to do with your father, Frída said?'

'That's right. She was *very* important to my father. And information has come to my attention since my poor father died that concerns me.'

'Information about her death.'

'Information about the death of the man who killed her.'

'You know who killed her?'

'I do.'

Magnus studied the woman opposite him. She could be a time-waster. Or a fantasist. She didn't *look* like a time-waster or fantasist.

'What do you do in England, Mrs Sugarman?' he asked.

'Louisa, please.'

'And I'm Magnus. You probably know we always use first names in Iceland.'

'Are you American? You speak perfect English. American English.'

'No, I'm an Icelander, but I spent many years there.'

Louisa nodded. 'To answer your question, I'm retired now. I was a lawyer. Not your sort of law, I'm afraid. Company law.'

'Which firm?' Magnus asked.

'Seabrook Renwick,' Louisa said.

'I've heard of it.' That was one of the big ones. Magnus's old girlfriend Colby had been a corporate lawyer in Boston and he had spent too much time with her ambitious lawyer friends, so he knew a bit about the big international law firms. They never got anywhere near a police station. 'Were you a partner, by any chance?'

'I was,' said Louisa, with a hint of a smile, acknowledging that she was establishing her credibility.

'You've come here to tell me a story,' Magnus said. 'So tell it.'

'My father's name was Tom Marks. He was a schoolmaster at a small prep school in Yorkshire – that's a kind of private elementary school. He saw war coming and joined the territorial army. He was shipped off to Iceland shortly after the British invaded in 1940 and was stationed in Hvalfjördur, not too far from the farm at Laxahóll.'

'Which is where Kristín lived.'

'That's correct. He met her. They fell in love. Or at least *he* fell in love with her. He says she loved him too, and I've no reason to doubt that.'

'He told you this?'

'Yes. A couple of years after my mother died. It was the late seventies; I had just graduated from university. He wanted to take me on a trip to Iceland with him, so we went for a week. We went to Hvalfjördur. He took me to Laxahóll – he was hoping to see Kristín's father, Hálfdán, but he had sold the farm a few years before.'

'Did you both go to Selvík?'

'Not then,' said Louisa. 'But I did go alone a few years ago. That's when I met Frída.'

'Sorry. Carry on,' said Magnus.

'So, on this trip, my father told me all about a girl he had met during the war, Kristín, how he had loved her and how he hoped to marry her and bring her back to England. This was all well before my mother, of course. Then one day she and her brother disappeared. No one knew why or where they had gone. They were at the farm alone, apart from

Kristín's son who was upstairs in bed. When their father came home, there was no sign of them.'

'That's what the police file from the time says,' said Magnus. 'But you say you know who killed them?'

'Yes. Or my father knew.'

'And who was it?'

'A British officer. Captain Neville Pybus-Smith.'

SIXTEEN

Magnus recognized the name from the old case file. 'How did your father know it was him?'

'He said this Pybus-Smith was obsessed with Kristín. He must have killed her and her brother, who was a communist. Pybus-Smith was in charge of intelligence on the island and he didn't like communists.'

'Is that it? Didn't your father have any evidence?'

'He had some, I think – I'm not sure exactly what – but it was nothing concrete. He was quite certain, right up to the end of his life.'

'Didn't he tell anyone? I mean, he believed this man had killed his girlfriend.'

'He did try to – I know he spoke to his commanding officer. But he didn't get anywhere. And that's where he admitted he didn't have any proper evidence. It was complicated by the fact that Pybus-Smith was leading the investigation on the part of the British authorities.'

'That's right. I read about him in the file. He didn't find anything.'

'Well, he wouldn't, would he?' Louisa sighed. 'Looking

back on it, I can see why Dad's commanding officer didn't want to pursue it. It must have sounded as if my father was jealous. And no one would have liked the idea of a British officer killing two civilians. So, without evidence . . .'

'No, I can see that,' said Magnus. He hesitated. Louisa noticed and waited.

Thelma had told him not to tell anyone about the bullet they had found. But this woman deserved to know the truth.

'Actually,' he said. 'There is some evidence now. If I tell you something, can you promise to keep it in strict confidence?'

'All right.'

Magnus couldn't decide whether the fact that Louisa was a lawyer meant he could or couldn't trust her. If he was her client or she had signed a non-disclosure agreement, certainly. But without those?

There was something about this woman: he trusted her. And she deserved to know the truth about her father, just as Magnus had deserved to know the truth about his own father.

'The bullets that killed them came out of the kind of revolver that was issued to British officers in 1940.'

Louisa sat back. Then she laughed. 'So Dad *was* right!'

'Did you doubt him?'

Louisa winced. 'Maybe. I mean, perhaps his commanding officer had a point. But this proves it.'

'Not quite,' said Magnus. 'It could have been another British officer. Or an Icelander who had gotten hold of a British weapon. But it certainly makes it much more likely it was Pybus-Smith.'

'Thank you for telling me, Magnus. I can assure you I'll keep it confidential.'

'I'd appreciate it. And it's interesting to hear your

father's views. But we won't be opening an investigation. It was all too long ago. Whoever did shoot them is long dead. This Captain Pybus-Smith, for example.'

'Oh, he's dead,' said Louisa. 'That's the reason why I flew here to talk to you.'

Magnus raised his eyebrows.

'Sir Neville Pybus-Smith, as he became, was murdered. Strangled in 1985 at his flat in Kensington – that's in London.'

'Did they catch the murderer?'

'They did. Or they thought they did. A black prostitute called Joyce Morgan. She had been to his house and they had indulged in an S&M session. You know what I mean by S&M? Sadomasochism?'

'We have that in America too,' Magnus said with a grin.

'The police assumed it had gone wrong. She was convicted of murder and was sentenced to life.'

'Did your father know?'

'Oh, yes. It was all over the papers at the time. We spoke about it. He admitted to me he was pleased that Pybus-Smith was dead although he knew he shouldn't have been.'

'I can understand that.'

'But the prostitute proclaimed her innocence. She said she'd been framed.'

'That doesn't mean anything,' said Magnus. 'Believe me.'

'Perhaps. But she had convincing reasons. A journalist called Amanda Wicker became interested in her story and wrote an article about it a few years later. According to her, the police knew that Joyce had left the block of flats before Pybus-Smith had died. But they hid the evidence.'

'Why?' Magnus didn't hide his scepticism.

'Because the chief inspector in charge of the case had a

grudge against her. Joyce had told a corruption investigation she had granted him sexual favours to avoid prosecution.'

Magnus became sceptical of his scepticism. That sounded all too plausible. Mind you, it was also plausible that the hooker had made the whole story up.

'Who knows?' he said.

'Exactly,' said Louisa. 'But what I found interesting in the article was that Joyce said she saw two men entering the building when she was leaving it.'

'Oh, yes?'

'They were speaking to each other in a foreign language.'

Magnus knew where this was going. 'Which language?'

'Joyce didn't know. She said it sounded like Swedish but she wasn't sure.'

'So it could have been Icelandic?'

'It's possible, isn't it?'

Magnus narrowed his eyes. 'Maybe. Some kind of revenge for Kristín and Marteinn's death?'

'Perhaps. Here. I've got a copy of the articles Amanda Wicker wrote.' She opened her bag and handed Magnus an envelope. 'They are in there. Oh, and there's this.'

She handed him an old black-and-white photograph.

It showed a tall, attractive woman in an Icelandic woollen hat with ear flaps, smiling at the camera. She was standing beside a motorcycle.

'That's her?' said Magnus.

'Yes,' said Louisa.

'I can see why your father liked her.'

'So can I.'

Magnus squinted. 'Is that Reykjavík in the background? They are just beneath Esja, aren't they, on Kollafjördur?'

Louisa nodded. 'We stopped there when we came here

on holiday. He showed me the exact spot and the photo. And then there is this.'

She smiled as she handed Magnus an exceedingly battered small book.

'An Icelandic–English dictionary?'

'That's right. Look in the front cover.'

Magnus carefully opened the book. There was a pencilled inscription on the first page in Icelandic:

Til Ara fróda.
Ég elska vitur ord thín.
Kristín

To Ari the Learned.
I love your wise words.
Kristín

'You know who Ari the Learned was?' Magnus asked with a smile. 'He wrote the *Íslendingabók*. Iceland's first history.'

'Don't I just. Dad told me all about him.'

A man after Magnus's own heart.

He returned the photograph and the dictionary to Louisa.

'OK,' he said. 'I must admit this is all very interesting. But I'm not sure what I can do about it. We have a murder in Iceland eighty-three years ago. The only surviving person involved was six at the time. And then another murder in a foreign country nearly forty years ago. My boss would never allow me to spend time on this, even if I wanted to.'

'A woman went to jail for a murder she didn't commit.'

'Possibly. Is she still alive? Is she still in jail? I'm not sure what life sentences actually mean in Britain, but I assume she's out by now.'

'I don't know,' Louisa admitted. 'The judge said she should serve a minimum of twenty years, so I assume you're right. According to the articles, she was thirty-four in 1985, so she would be seventy-something now. And if she didn't commit the crime, perhaps those two men did? Perhaps they were Icelanders? They could still be alive.'

'They could.'

'Look, it's a question of justice. If that poor woman was wrongly imprisoned by a crooked policeman, then something should be done about it. Even if it is nearly forty years later. Don't you agree?'

Magnus frowned.

'I have a slightly overdeveloped sense of justice,' Louisa said with a smile. 'Dad always used to say my motto as a little girl was "It's not fair!" I suppose that's why I became a lawyer.'

Magnus nodded. 'That's why I became a detective.' In his case, it was because no one had been able to solve his own father's murder, which had blown Magnus's life apart when he was twenty. Magnus had eventually succeeded, but it had taken him fourteen years. In that period, as a Boston homicide detective, he had done all he could to bring murderers of other people's fathers, mothers, daughters and sons to justice.

He was still doing it in Iceland.

'All right,' he said. 'But even if the murderer turned out to be an Icelander living in Iceland, this is outside our jurisdiction.'

'That's why I came here. Naturally, that's your answer, and one you would have given me in an email response if I had sent you one. And do you think the Met is going to reopen a case on the suspicion that one of their number framed a prostitute forty years ago? But someone should do something.'

She was right.

'Shall I talk to your boss?' she said.

'No. Don't do that,' said Magnus. 'I guarantee that won't work.'

'I plan to speak to that journalist. She was young in the 1990s – she's still writing. I expect she'll be interested in this.'

Magnus expected she would too. And if she was, that would produce exactly the kind of furore that Thelma wanted to avoid.

But this competent, down-to-earth British lawyer, whom Magnus was beginning to like, was right. It *was* a question of justice.

He had eventually found justice for his father. She had a right to find justice for hers.

'Look,' he said. 'Officially, I know I won't be able to help you. But I understand what you're saying. How long are you in Iceland?'

'I don't know. A week? I'd like to go to Kristín's funeral, if she's having one. And I'd like to visit Hvalfjördur and maybe Kristín's son if he's still alive. You said he was still alive?'

'He is.'

'Can you give me his address?'

'Not without his permission.' Magnus relented. 'But it's not that hard to find someone's address in Iceland with an online directory if you've got the postcode. Especially if I were to tell you I went to see him in Grafarholt – that's postcode 113. Which I won't.' Magnus thought a moment. 'If you do find him, don't tell him about the bullet, remember?'

'I remember,' said Louisa.

'All right. Give me your cell phone number and tell me where you're staying and I will get in touch with you if I find out anything relevant.' Magnus smiled. 'And I *will* ask the questions.'

Louisa returned his smile. 'I believe you will.'

After he had seen Louisa out of the station, Magnus took a look at the article she had left him.

It was from a British newspaper called *The Independent*, dated March 1990, with the byline Amanda Wicker.

The article outlined the case much as Louisa had described it. There was more detail on Sir Neville Pybus-Smith, describing him as a seventy-five-year-old merchant banker who was on the board of a couple of large British companies. He had a wife and two adult daughters, one of whom was married to a mildly famous TV actor. Joyce Morgan had been born in Jamaica and arrived in Britain with her parents when she was ten. She had two sons of her own.

Her story was that Pybus-Smith was a regular client, that despite his age he had a penchant for bondage and that she had visited him for a one-hour 'session' at eight-thirty on the evening of 12 March 1985. The session had gone without a hitch, she had been paid and she had left at 9.45 p.m. She had seen two men entering the building, speaking some kind of Scandinavian language. Another resident of the building had seen her leave and was able to corroborate the time.

The prosecution at her trial claimed that she had murdered Pybus-Smith at about 9.30 p.m., strangling him, perhaps as part of a sex game gone wrong. The police had been unable to find the two Scandinavian men and doubted their existence.

Joyce had claimed she had been framed. She said she had acted as an informant a couple of years before in a corruption investigation, where she had accused a number of police officers of turning a blind eye to prostitution in exchange for sex. Her arrest for the murder was payback for that. Not just payback, it was sending a message to anyone else who might consider turning on their police protectors.

The prosecution pointed out that the corruption investigation had got nowhere because the evidence from Joyce and others like her had been shown to be baseless. She was only bringing it up now to get off the murder charge. The judge agreed and had ruled Joyce's claims inadmissible in court.

Amanda Wicker had discovered that there had been a call to a minicab company from Pybus-Smith's phone at his flat at 9.47 p.m. That phone call had not been mentioned at the trial. Wicker had been in touch with the minicab company, who had told her that Pybus-Smith had indeed booked a cab from his flat to Heathrow the following morning. The driver remembered waiting for him outside and him not showing up.

At the trial, it had emerged that Pybus-Smith had suffered a blow to his head, probably just before he died. This wasn't explained by the prosecution, and the defence had made little of it – in Amanda Wicker's opinion they should have. But it didn't fit with a sex game gone wrong.

The journalist had contacted the police to ask them about the phone call to the minicab company, but they had simply not responded.

Magnus did some hasty googling. There were two more

articles in *The Independent* about the case, the last one, dated January 1991, more or less admitting defeat.

Magnus didn't know what to make of the articles. The conviction sounded fishy. He had heard that the London Metropolitan Police had had corruption problems in the seventies and eighties, as had many other police departments around the world, including Boston's. But Joyce Morgan could just be trying it on. And there might be a reasonable explanation for the non-disclosure of the phone call to the minicab firm. Or perhaps the witness who said they saw Joyce leaving the building at 9.45 p.m. had got the time wrong and it had been later. Joyce had killed Pybus-Smith at 9.50 p.m. – after the phone call – and then left.

That didn't really make sense. If indeed Pybus-Smith had died accidentally, that would imply he had made the call while he was in the middle of whatever sex games he and Joyce Morgan were playing. It seemed extremely unlikely that he would have booked the cab before the sex session had ended.

What if Joyce Morgan was telling the truth? What if those two men *were* Icelanders? What if they had entered the block of flats at 9.45 p.m. that evening, knocked at Pybus-Smith's door just after he had called a minicab, and killed him?

Why had they killed him?

Because he had shot Kristín and Marteinn forty-five years before.

Was that too many what-ifs?

Probably. And forty-five years was an awfully long time to wait before taking revenge.

There was no point in asking the London police for the file. He could try speaking to Amanda Wicker. She might have found more evidence that she was unable to publish at the time.

But that would open the can of worms that Thelma wanted to remain closed.

He should speak to Gudni again. At the very least, he should do that.

Tomorrow.

SEVENTEEN

Ingileif wasn't home when Magnus eventually got back to her apartment in Vesturbaer on the hill above the Old Harbour, but Ási was.

'Hi, Dad,' the boy said. Magnus grinned. Having a little boy call him 'Dad' never got old. Though Ási wasn't that little any more. He was only ten, but he was one of the tallest in his class.

'Where's Mum?'

'She said she'll be back at seven-thirty. Did you see the Patriots won last night? Beat the Steelers seventeen to fourteen.'

'I did,' said Magnus. Father and son spent a companionable quarter of an hour talking about football, while Magnus put some pasta on to boil.

Magnus wasn't sure that Ási was genuinely interested in football, or any other sport for that matter. But since Magnus had arrived on the scene, his son had made an effort to find out about the Red Sox and the Patriots. It touched Magnus greatly that Ási would go to all that effort to find a connection with his father, but he sometimes felt guilty that it ought to be the other way around. One day, Magnus would take him to Foxboro to see the Patriots. Would Ási like it? There was only one way to find out.

Ingileif arrived a little after seven, and, as always, Magnus's heart gave a little flutter to see her. She looked happy.

'I think I'm going to get that fishing lodge in the East Fjords,' she said as she began to lay the table. 'Hjörtur wants me to fly out there next week. They want rustic-modern rather than rustic-quaint. That's something I can do.'

'That's great.' Ingileif's interior-design business had gone into hibernation during the pandemic, but the post-COVID tourist boom was bringing her plenty of opportunities. She had a good reputation and excellent contacts among Iceland's artistic community, but she was careful to avoid big and bland jobs, however remunerative they were. An upscale fishing lodge would suit her down to the ground.

'Any news on those two bodies they found yesterday?' she asked. 'I heard something about it on the radio.'

Magnus told her a bit about the case, avoiding too much detail on the skeletons, for Ási's benefit. After dinner, Ási went off to his room to practise his violin. He needed no encouragement – he loved the instrument, and he was getting pretty good at it. Magnus and Ingileif sat on the sofa with a beer and a glass of wine.

Ingileif's apartment was tasteful in the extreme. Good art, good glass, good ceramics, elegant lilies. A wonderful view of the fishing boats in the Old Harbour between Vesturbaer's rooftops. Plain but warm wooden floorboards. No clutter, apart from a dozen strategically placed candles. No stuff.

It was her apartment; there was very little of Magnus in

it. He had never had much stuff, but half of what he did have had been packed in a couple of boxes and stored in his old landlord Tryggvi Thór's basement when he had moved in with Ingileif. Magnus was happy with that; he didn't want to mess up her lovely apartment, and she had at least designed an elegant bookcase for his books, which was what he cared about most. But it meant he felt like a visitor. A guest.

Maybe he was happy with that too?

'How's Vigdís's mother?' Ingileif asked.

Magnus winced. 'Not good. Turned out she *was* drunk. But worse than that, after Vigdís kicked her out of her apartment, Audur drove home. And hit someone.'

'Oh, no! Was she arrested?'

'No. Hit and run. And Vigdís saw it.'

'Did she say anything?'

'Nope.'

Ingileif looked at Magnus, understanding. 'And you think she should have done?'

Magnus nodded. 'I do.'

'Is the guy she hit OK?'

'Apparently. But her mother isn't, clearly. Who knows what will happen next time she runs someone over?'

'You can't expect her to turn in her own mother, Magnús!'

Magnus shrugged. 'They do this to you, alcoholics. They force you to become their allies. You have to stand up to them.'

'You're not going to report her yourself, are you?'

'No,' said Magnus. 'Of course not. And I do feel sorry for Vigdís. She believes Audur hadn't touched a drop for a year.'

'Was Erla OK?'

'Yes, Erla's fine.'

They sipped their drinks in silence. Silence, that is, apart from the Beethoven minuet drifting in from Ási's room.

'So? Have you decided when we get married?' Ingileif asked.

Magnus had expected the question. He couldn't dodge it, and Ingileif deserved an answer. 'I don't want to get married. Or I do. But not now. Not for a couple of years.'

Ingileif frowned, and Magnus could see she was about to come out with a sharp retort, but she controlled herself. 'I don't understand why not, Magnús. I really don't understand why not.'

'Neither did I. I had to think about it.'

'And?'

She had a right to know, but it was going to be difficult to tell her.

'I think if we stay as we are for a few years, then we'll be more certain it's the right thing to do.'

'What does that mean, Magnús? Don't you trust me? The whole point of this is to demonstrate that we trust each other.'

'Of course I trust you. Now.'

'Now? What do you mean *now*?'

Magnus took a deep breath. 'I mean, you change, Ingileif. That's one of the things I love about you, but . . .'

'But what?'

'You married Hannes, didn't you? When you did that, that was a commitment, wasn't it? And then you started seeing other men. You did the same thing with me before. You might do it again. I know you don't mean to now. Just like Vigdís's mother didn't mean to drink again.'

Colour rose to Ingileif's cheeks. 'Oh, so you think I'm some kind of sex addict, do you?'

'No,' said Magnus. 'I'm sorry, Audur was a bad comparison. But I do want to be sure you don't walk off again.'

Ingileif looked as if she was about to explode. But she lowered her voice. 'Don't you see, Magnús? That's the whole point. I *have* changed. And I want to stay changed. With you.'

There was anger, but also sadness in her eyes. 'It *was* different when I married Hannes. It wasn't just that I didn't love him as much as I love you. I went into it with a different mindset. He wanted to get married and I thought marriage would be kind of fun. It's true I didn't take it too seriously – I had a couple of flings but they didn't mean anything. *He* was the one who ran off with someone else. And then, when he wanted to come back, I decided I wanted to be with you. Properly.'

'I know.'

'Don't you believe me?' Her grey eyes looked into his, beseeching.

'Of course I do,' Magnus said.

'Well then?'

'I just don't want to have the same thing happen to me as happened to Hannes. Again.'

Ingileif shook her head. She looked down into her empty wine glass.

'Is that the only reason?' she muttered.

'Yes, it is,' said Magnus.

He waited for Ingileif to speak. She looked up. 'What about Erla?'

'What about Erla?'

She took out her phone and fiddled with it. 'Look at this,' she said.

Magnus took the phone. It was a picture of Erla on a swing in a playground in Hafnarfjördur, taken when Magnus and Ingileif had been round to lunch with Vigdís the previous month. It was a close-up. She had a big smile on her face.

'OK,' said Magnus.

Ingileif took her phone back and fiddled some more. 'Now look at this.'

It was a picture of a red-haired toddler of about the same age having just as much fun on another swing.

'That's Ási, isn't it?' Magnus hadn't met Ási until he was three years older, but it was clearly their son.

'Don't you think they look similar?'

Magnus swallowed. 'No. Erla's skin is darker – Ási's is pale. Her hair is black, Ási's is red. So no, they don't look similar.'

'Oh, come on, Magnús, of course they do! Look at that smile. Look at the nose.'

Magnus resolutely shook his head. He returned Ingileif's phone. 'What are you saying?'

'I'm saying they could be brother and sister. Or half-brother and -sister.'

'You think I'm Erla's father?'

'Who is her father?'

Magnus shrugged. 'Not me.'

'Magnús. You have form for fathering children you know nothing about.'

'That's hardly my fault,' Magnus said. 'You never told me about Ási. I had no idea he even existed!'

Ingileif's eyes were hard. 'Have you slept with Vigdís?'

Magnus hesitated. Ingileif noticed. 'No.'

'No? Magnús?'

Magnus knew this wasn't the time for half-truths. Or half-lies.

'No. But I did kiss her. Once. Over ten years ago. When you left to go to Germany. We got drunk. It was a mistake. We never did it again. We never talk about it.'

'You never told me about that,' Ingileif said.

'No,' said Magnus.

'You were drunk?'

'Yes. We both were. We both regretted it.'

'And it was just a kiss?'

'Yeah. But not just a peck on the cheek.'

'I see.' Ingileif nodded to herself. 'I was doing some calculations. Erla's about eighteen months old, right?'

'I think so, maybe a little younger.'

'Which means she must have been conceived in the summer of 2021.'

'Does it?'

'When you and Vigdís went out drinking and you came home at five in the morning. You know, when your brother and his friends came over to Iceland.'

'I didn't sleep with Vigdís,' Magnus said.

Ingileif showed her phone to Magnus. 'And you still say Ási doesn't look like Erla?'

Magnus nodded. 'I don't think so.'

But the little boy did look a lot like the little girl. He knew that and Ingileif knew that.

'I don't believe you, Magnús. I don't think it's me you can't trust.' She glared at him, sadness once again tingeing her anger. 'I think it's you.'

EIGHTEEN

The radiocarbon-dating report from the Anthropology Department of the University of Iceland was waiting for Magnus when he logged on to his computer in the morning.

The results were frustrating. You needed soft tissue to date time of death, but in this case that had long decayed. Teeth could be very roughly dated to the time they were formed. The age of a skeleton at death was important as was how and in what type of ground it had been buried.

Variables piled upon variables. The only thing the report could state for sure was that the victims had been buried before the 1950s when the prevalence of carbon-14 in the world's atmosphere had risen dramatically following a spate of nuclear bomb tests.

So 1940 was possible as a date of death. And, more importantly, these were not recent murders.

But they still needed the DNA analysis for a definite ID.

Vigdís arrived, looking worn out.

Was it Erla? Audur? Magnus didn't know, and, given

their conversation about Vigdís's mother the previous day, he decided not to ask.

He briefed her on the radiocarbon report and his discussion with Louisa Sugarman the previous afternoon.

'Can we get the British police file on Pybus-Smith's murder?' Vigdís asked.

'I doubt it,' said Magnus. 'An investigation in the 1980s? Not just that, but one that was questioned in the press? The investigating officers will have long retired, and if they haven't, they certainly won't want to talk to us about it. Europol will take forever and then the Brits will probably just say no.'

There was an international mechanism for sharing such information through Europol and Interpol, but it was cumbersome. Magnus often had better luck using informal channels with a direct phone call to the police officer involved in an investigation overseas, but that wouldn't work in this case.

'So, what about these two Scandinavian men? Were they real?'

'Could be,' said Magnus. 'It's an odd thing to make up. But it's not clear to me whether they were seen before or after Pybus-Smith was murdered. They could just have been visiting someone else in the building.'

'Is it worth seeing Gudni again? See if he knows anything?'

Magnus's phone rang.

Assault outside a house in Kópavogur. A sixteen-year-old boy had been beaten up by intruders leaving his parents' house on his way to school. He was now in hospital.

Magnus had a sinking feeling about this one as he set off, taking Vigdís with him.

The case was as Magnus feared. The kid had been

attacked by a large guy who had knocked him about and trodden on his phone. Not stolen it. Destroyed it.

The boy, who was conscious in hospital with a broken collarbone, swore blind that he had no idea why he had been attacked, that it must have been a mugging. His description of the thug was vague in the extreme: 'big' was the only adjective he was confident of.

The boy's mother, who was with him, was distraught.

Magnus and Vigdís both knew what had happened. The kid owed money for drugs and hadn't paid. The mother probably didn't even know that her son took drugs. The kid was terrified of both the dealers whom he had left unpaid and his parents in case they found out what had really happened.

Vigdís took the mother to one side, and Magnus talked to the boy.

In six years' time, could this be Ási? Would Magnus be the parent fussing in the hospital?

Would he trust Ási if he swore blind he had never touched drugs or bought from dealers? Probably not, given what Magnus had seen in his professional life. Would Ingileif?

Probably.

'Why can't I be in there with him?' the woman asked Vigdís. She was in her mid-forties, a little heavy, with long blonde hair. She was tense, worried, but also willing to fight for her child.

They were in a quiet corner of the corridor of the hospital. Magnus was asking the kid awkward questions, questions which he probably wouldn't answer, and which he definitely wouldn't answer if his mother was with him.

'Has your son ever had trouble with drugs?' Vigdís asked her, as blandly as she could.

'Drugs? No, of course not. Doddi has never taken drugs. How can you ask that?'

Vigdís searched the woman's eyes for a hint of doubt, and found it. The woman turned away from her. Vigdís persisted; she wanted to warn the mother gently how this was going to go.

'We have had a couple of similar incidents over the last few months,' Vigdís said. 'And we would like to catch the gang who are responsible. So more kids aren't beaten up.'

'It was a mugging. It's obvious. Doddi is only sixteen! He's never been in trouble with the police, or even at school.' She hesitated. 'Well, not much trouble.'

Vigdís had checked LÖKE, the police database, and the mother was correct about that, at least as far as the police were concerned. 'Let's just wait for my colleague, shall we?' she said.

Her phone rang.

She glanced at the woman, stood up and moved away as she answered. 'Hello?'

'Hi, Vigdís, it's Lúdvík. Listen, I've got some bad news. You know that jogger who was hit outside your place on Tuesday?'

'Yes?' Vigdís felt her throat tighten, as if to trap the panic she could feel rising in her chest.

'He died. Last night.'

'What? But I thought he was OK?'

'So did I. He spent the night in hospital, and they didn't spot anything, so they let him go in the morning. But it turns out there was bleeding in his brain. He called an ambulance with a bad headache last night, but by the time they got him to the hospital he was dead.'

'But they were supposed to observe him, right?' said Vigdís, unsuccessfully trying to control the panic. 'Why didn't they spot it? Didn't they do a brain scan?'

'I don't know,' said Lúdvík. 'I guess not.'

'Why not?' demanded Vigdís.

'I have no idea,' said Lúdvík. Vigdís picked up a hint of suspicion in his reply. She had to get control of herself. Immediately.

'Of course you don't,' she said, her voice steadier. 'I'm sorry. It's a bit of a shock. I was just pleased that he was OK, and now, suddenly, he's not.'

'I know,' said Lúdvík. 'I spoke to him – he was a nice guy. A devoted girlfriend. Two devoted parents. It was a shock to all of them.'

'I bet it was,' said Vigdís.

'Anyway. It means I need to take a formal statement from you.'

Vigdís's heart sank. 'Of course.'

'Are you at the station now?'

Vigdís glanced at the mother, who was watching her closely. 'No. I'm at the National Hospital. I'll probably be back by lunchtime.'

'Good. I'll come by and take a statement from you then.'

'If you can wait till this evening, we can do it at my place,' Vigdís said, playing for time. That would be more convenient for Lúdvík, who was based in Hafnarfjördur.

'No, I'll come your way. You're the only witness.'

'OK,' said Vigdís. 'I'll call you when I'm back at the station.'

She hung up.

'Bad news?' asked the woman, with a look of concern.

Vigdís nodded. 'Very.'

. . .

Gudni smiled as Jimmy Greaves blasted the ball into the back of the net past the Burnley goalkeeper.

It was one of a series of DVDs in Gudni's collection. His son Bjarni had given him a set of Tottenham Hotspur's six televised FA Cup final victories for Christmas a few years ago. Comfort fare. He needed it now, to take his mind off all those thoughts that were swirling around his brain since the police's visit the day before.

But, as Burnley restarted the game, his thoughts returned to his mother. And his father, and his grandfather and uncle and aunt and all those people who had looked after him and were now gone. His father he couldn't remember and his mother only barely. But Grandpa and Uncle Siggi had done a good job bringing him up at Laxahóll, as had Sunna when she had married Uncle Siggi. Fortunately, Gudni was well out of the house and married himself when Siggi ran away with Frída from Selvík, but perhaps because of that he had been able to maintain contact with his uncle, who was only twelve years older than him.

But even Uncle Siggi had been dead over twenty years. Elísabet, Gudni's beloved wife, was gone now too.

The Burnley winger crossed the ball, but their centre forward nodded it wide, as Gudni knew he would, having seen him miss at that point in the game a dozen times before.

Gudni would be ninety in six months' time. What was the point? Shouldn't he just turn up his toes? Except you couldn't turn up your toes, just like that.

He needed to shake himself out of this. There were new people in his family. His son and his two daughters. His six grandchildren. Maybe great-grandchildren soon. Even Jón, Siggi's son, and his children.

Would they care if he turned up his toes?

They might. A bit.

The entryphone buzzed. Gudni glanced at his watch: it was not yet ten o'clock. He heaved himself out of his armchair and checked the tiny screen. Looked like a woman: a woman he didn't recognize.

He buzzed her in.

A minute later she rang the doorbell to his flat and he opened the door. She was blonde, in her sixties, shrewd eyes and a friendly smile. Foreign.

'Hello,' she said. 'Gudni Thorsteinsson?' My name is Louisa Sugarman. Do you speak English?'

'I do,' said Gudni.

The woman smiled. 'Good. May I come in?'

Gudni wasn't sure.

'I'd like to speak to you about your mother.'

Gudni still wasn't sure. But his curiosity over why this British woman would know or care about his mother overwhelmed his caution.

'All right. Come in. Would you like some coffee?'

Gudni had set himself up with a thermos for the morning and fussed over mugs as he poured one for himself and one for his guest.

Louisa noticed the TV and paused to watch for a few seconds. 'Nineteen sixty-one FA Cup final?' she said. 'Or is it sixty-two?'

'Sixty-two! How did you know?'

'I'm a lifelong Spurs fan.' She took the mug from Gudni's shaking hand. 'I had to be, given my father.'

Gudni shuffled back to his armchair. So that was it.

He sipped his coffee. 'Tom?'

'That's right!' said the woman with a broad smile. 'Tom Marks. Do you remember him?'

Gudni nodded. 'Yes. But I was only six when I knew him.'

The woman reached into her handbag and pulled out two photographs. She handed one to Gudni. 'Is that you?'

It was the one of the British soldier kicking the ball to a little boy.

'That's me,' said Gudni. He couldn't resist a smile. 'And that's him. And you are his daughter?'

'I am. Here.' She handed him the second photo. Gudni wasn't surprised to see his mother and the iron stallion.

He nodded. 'I have both of these,' he said. His heart was churning. He felt a surge of warmth towards this woman, almost kinship.

On the other hand . . .

'She was very beautiful, your mother, wasn't she?'

Gudni smiled. 'I remember her as beautiful. I only have a few photographs of her. Over time, she has become, I don't know, black and white?'

'I'm sorry you lost her so young.'

The woman seemed to mean it. Her face spoke of genuine sympathy.

'I assume your own father must be dead by now?'

'Oh, yes. He lasted until the age of seventy-eight. He talked about your mother a lot. Especially after my own mother died.'

'You know they've found her body?' Gudni said. 'Along with my uncle?'

'Yes. That's why I'm here.'

He thought as much.

'Gudni, I'd like to speak to you about another British officer from the war. I don't know whether you will remember him. Captain Neville Pybus-Smith?'

NINETEEN

Magnus was returning to his desk from the men's room when he noticed Vigdís in a conference room speaking to a cop he recognized from Hafnarfjördur – Lúdvík. It looked like the cop was taking a statement.

The kid had stayed quiet, refusing to admit that he knew of any reason why he had been beaten up by a stranger. Magnus and Vigdís had spoken to him and his mother together. Magnus outlined their suspicions, which were met by vehement denials from mother and son. Magnus simply pointed out that if indeed the boy had started taking drugs, now was a good time to stop.

They had heard him. That was all he could do.

The police wanted an ID of the thug – the boy's description was useless. Two officers were knocking on doors looking for witnesses. Magnus intended to send Vigdís out to join them.

'Was that the hit and run?' Magnus asked Vigdís as she returned to her desk. She looked shaken.

She nodded.

'Did you tell him what really happened?'

Vigdís avoided Magnus's eyes and shook her head.

Magnus sighed. 'Don't you think you should have?'

Vigdís looked up at him, anguish ravaging her face. She glanced around. The nearby desks were empty: there was no one in earshot at that moment.

'He died.'

'The jogger?'

Vigdís nodded miserably.

'But you said he was OK?'

'Bleeding in the brain. The hospital didn't spot it even though they kept him in for observation.'

'And you *still* didn't tell Lúdvík you saw it.'

Vigdís shook her head. 'I couldn't. It's my mother.'

Magnus felt a surge of anger. 'You idiot! You have to tell them. Have you just signed a witness statement that's false?'

Vigdís nodded.

'What do you expect me to do? Keep quiet?'

Vigdís sighed. 'You do whatever you have to do, Magnús. I just can't shop my own mother. I'm sorry.'

'Oh, great.' Part of Magnus felt sympathy towards Vigdís. He knew what she had been through over the years with her mother. If she admitted what she had seen, that would definitely mean more prison time for Audur.

And so it damn well should.

A familiar rage bubbled up inside him as he thought of his own mother. The woman who had abandoned him first to drink and then in that car crash. Who had left him and Ollie to years of hell at the hands of her parents, their grandparents, at that farm in Snaefellsnes.

Magnus had never forgiven her for that. And he wasn't about to forgive Audur either, for ruining her daughter's career, his friend's career.

He fought to control his anger. 'I'm not going to do this

for you, Vigdís,' he said. 'You have to go back to Lúdvík and tell him what really happened.'

'I won't.'

'You will. I'll give you twenty-four hours to think about it. Then I'll talk to him myself.'

Vigdís opened her mouth to protest. Then, her eyes moist, she turned away from him, grabbing her coat. 'I'll see how the guys in Kópavogur are getting on with the witnesses.'

Magnus watched her go. Would he carry out his threat if she didn't correct the record? Damn right he would.

But he was confident that once she had had time to think it over, she would do the right thing. Magnus didn't give a toss for Audur – she had just killed a man.

But he did care about Vigdís.

His phone buzzed. It was the front desk. Two people to see him: Gudni Thorsteinsson and his son Bjarni.

Both men seemed nervous as Magnus brought them cups of coffee and sat them down in an interview room.

Bjarni appeared to be about sixty, tall, slim except for a little paunch above his belt, short bristles of thin blond hair edging a shiny scalp. He was wearing the uniform of a certain kind of Icelandic businessman: a black T-shirt, expensive jacket, jeans and pointed leather shoes.

He looked anxious. His father looked unhappy.

'How can I help you?' Magnus said with a smile, in an attempt to ease the tension.

Gudni grabbed his thumb and started picking at a nail. He had had a certain vigour the first time Magnus had met him, but now he just looked very old and exhausted. Wisps of long grey hair strayed haphazardly across the wrinkles of his face. His eyes, angled downwards, avoided Magnus's.

'I haven't been strictly honest with you.'

'I see,' said Magnus, careful to sound encouraging rather than angry. 'People are not always honest with us. But if they straighten things out as soon as they can, things usually go better for everyone.'

Gudni flashed Magnus a quick nervous smile. 'That's what I'm hoping.'

Magnus was silent. So was Gudni. He was really digging into his thumbnail. His son was watching impatiently.

'What is it you didn't tell me that you should have?' prompted Magnus.

Gudni glanced upwards at him quickly before averting his eyes again.

'Mum's death. Uncle Marteinn's. You know I said I didn't see them?'

'Yes?'

'Well, I did.'

Magnus nodded. Gently does it. Seeing his mother shot would be a painful memory for a six-year-old boy, even eighty-three years later.

'What happened?' he said.

Gudni glanced at his son, who nodded back to him in encouragement.

'A British soldier came to the farm to see Mum. It was late afternoon, just beginning to get dark. Grandpa wasn't there, and Uncle Marteinn was out on the farm somewhere. Mum told me to go upstairs and play in the bedroom and she gave the soldier some coffee.

'I heard them going outside together. A few minutes

later I heard Uncle Marteinn shouting and then a loud shot. I rushed to my window. It overlooked the barns.

'The soldier came out of the hay barn, and then Uncle Marteinn came out too with Mum, who was crying. Uncle Marteinn was carrying a shotgun.'

Gudni paused. Pressed his thumb against his quivering lower lip. 'The man shot Uncle Marteinn with his pistol. Then he shot Mum.'

Gudni was speaking so quietly that Magnus could barely hear him. Bjarni clasped his arm.

'I'm sorry to ask you this, but do you remember where the man shot your uncle and your mother? I mean whereabouts on their bodies?'

Gudni shut his eyes tight. A tear leaked out and ran down his cheek. Bjarni glared at Magnus, admonishing him for causing his father the pain.

Eventually, Gudni nodded. 'He shot Uncle Marteinn in the chest. And then he shot Mum in the . . . in the . . .'

'Yes?'

Gudni took a breath. 'In the head. The forehead.'

That fitted with what the forensics people had found at the scene. More importantly, it was information that the police had withheld from the press or anyone else.

Gudni really had seen what he said he had seen.

'Why didn't you tell us this before?'

Now Gudni met Magnus's eyes. 'I was terrified. The soldier looked up from the farmyard and he saw me at my window. I hid under the bed. But he came back into the house and up to my room. He found me right away.'

Gudni swallowed. 'He knew I'd seen what he had done. I thought he was going to kill me right then. But he didn't. He just indicated that I should keep quiet or he would shoot me.'

'Indicated?'

'Yes. Put his finger to his lips. Pointed his gun at me. I knew what he meant. I knew if I said anything he would come and find me and he would kill me just like he had killed my mother. So I kept quiet. I told Grandpa I was in bed asleep and I hadn't heard anything. And I said the same thing to the policemen.'

'That was then. What about now? Why didn't you tell me what had really happened now?'

'I decided the best idea was to bury what I'd seen and keep it buried. And that's what I did. Until now.'

'Why now?'

'A British woman came to see me. Her name was Louisa Sugarman. Her father was a man called Tom who liked my mother. I remember him. She talked to me about a Captain Neville something-or-other who she said had killed Mum and Uncle Marteinn.'

'Did you tell her what you had seen?'

Gudni shook his head. 'No.'

'Why not?'

'Because it wasn't this Neville man who shot my mother.'

'Who was it, then?'

'It was Louisa's father. Tom.'

TWENTY

As Bjarni led his father out of the police station, Magnus turned to the window behind him, let his eyes rest on the familiar hulk of Esja on the other side of Kollafjördur and pondered what to do next.

Bjarni had asked when they could hold the funeral, and Magnus had said that the radiocarbon dating was inconclusive and they would have to wait until the DNA analysis came back from Sweden before they had a firm enough ID for the district magistrate to release the body for burial.

But, thinking about it, Gudni's testimony was pretty conclusive. He had seen his mother shot in the head and his uncle shot in the chest. Carbon dating was clear that the bones were from before 1950.

The bones couldn't belong to anyone else. He would talk to the magistrate. Gudni could bury his mother.

That left the problem of what to do about Louisa Sugarman. The knowledge that it was her beloved father who had shot Kristín and Marteinn all those years ago would devastate her. Magnus was tempted to leave her in the dark. But Gudni's testimony would have to be recorded since it was key to identifying the bodies. Louisa was a lawyer and she was determined: she would find out what Gudni had testified.

Better if Magnus told her right away.

The Airbnb address she had given him was on Hverfisgata, up the hill from the police station. Not far. This was a message to be delivered in person, not on the phone.

He was lucky to catch her: she was just heading out for a walk. The Airbnb was an old one-bedroom flat in a building clad in deep-red corrugated metal. The ground floor was occupied by an outdoor-clothing store.

She offered him a cup of tea, but he asked for coffee. They sat down in the small living room. It was minimally furnished with a blue sofa and armchair, a TV and a pine table and chairs standing on weathered undulating floorboards. A large abstract painting of blacks and reds dominated the wall behind the table, somehow evoking a volcanic eruption.

'You have something to tell me,' she said. 'And I can see from your expression it's not good.'

'Gudni came in to see us just now. He said you spoke with him this morning?'

'Yes. I found Gudni's address on *já.is*, and I went round to see him today.'

'And he didn't say who he thought had killed his mother?'

'No. I told him about my father and Kristín, and how my father believed Captain Pybus-Smith had killed her and her brother. Then I told him Pybus-Smith had himself been murdered in 1985.'

'And how did he respond?'

'He seemed dazed. Confused. I don't know – it was hard to tell. I had meant to ask him whether he had been in

London when Pybus-Smith was killed, but I didn't have the heart. It all seemed too much for him to take in. I was thinking maybe I should see him again and ask him once he has had a chance to digest what I told him the first time. Or maybe not. Maybe I'll just leave it.'

'The thing is,' said Magnus, 'it turns out that Gudni did see who shot his mother.'

Louisa opened her eyes. 'And it was Pybus-Smith?'

Magnus shook his head. 'I'm sorry to say it was your father.'

'What?' Louisa sat stunned. 'What?' she repeated.

'That's what he said.'

'He must be mistaken. I did the numbers: he must be eighty-nine. He's old; he's confused. He's just got it wrong.'

'He described how Kristín and Marteinn were shot, one in the head and one in the chest. We hadn't released that information to anyone. He must have seen it.'

'That makes no sense at all.'

'I'm sorry,' Magnus said.

'But Dad loved her! He told me so many times he loved her. Why would he say that if he'd killed her?'

Magnus shrugged. 'I've seen a bunch of murders in my career, a lot more in America than here. And when a young woman is murdered it's often a husband or a boyfriend or a lover who killed her.'

'Why would he do that? What possible reason could he have?'

'I don't know,' said Magnus. 'And I'm not going to guess. It was more than eighty years ago. Gudni was six. We have no way of knowing.'

'My father wouldn't kill anyone! You never knew him. He didn't lose his temper. He was reliable, good in a crisis. I can't imagine him as a murderer.'

'Then don't,' said Magnus. Magnus was impressed by Louisa. She was driven by a sense of justice as acute as Magnus's. She had come all the way to Iceland because she had believed that a woman she didn't even know had been wrongly convicted. She was clearly a strong woman, but some of that strength would have come from her father, whom she had evidently admired all her life. To learn that this man who had given her so much was in fact a murderer must undermine everything she believed, everything she was.

This could break her. And that wasn't right.

'I know it's going to be very hard,' Magnus said. 'Just trust your instincts. We're not going to launch an investigation. We need Gudni's testimony to confirm that the bodies do indeed belong to Kristín and Marteinn, but nobody needs to make a fuss about it.'

'What about the press?'

Yes, what about the press? 'I know my boss, the detective superintendent, is very keen that the press don't get hold of the idea that these two were shot by a British officer. That's one of the reasons why we withheld the details of how they were killed. Gudni's testimony is not conclusive proof, and also he has been reluctant to talk about it for the last eighty years. So we may be able to keep the details quiet.'

'But you think my father shot them?'

'I don't know,' said Magnus.

'If he killed her, why would he talk to me about her so much? Take me on a trip with him to Iceland?' She sat up straight and shook her head. 'No. I just don't believe it.'

'All right,' said Magnus. 'I can understand that. But I know you were considering going to Kristín's funeral. You might want to rethink that.'

Louisa sighed. 'You're probably right. And thanks for telling me.' Although her face was set firm, Magnus could see in the trembling of the corners of her lips and the desperation in her eyes that she was struggling against the crushing weight of the news she had just heard.

'I'll leave you now,' said Magnus. 'I am sorry.'

Louisa didn't respond; she just stared at that big painting of black and red.

TWENTY-ONE

Ingileif was less cool towards him than Magnus had expected that evening.

'I bumped into your old landlord in the street this afternoon. He asked after you.'

'Tryggvi Thór? How is he?'

'He looked old.'

'He is old. He's ancient.'

'Yeah, but he looked really old. Like he might be ill.'

'I hope not.' Tryggvi Thór was a former cop with whom Magnus had lodged for several years. They had got on surprisingly well.

'When was the last time you saw him?'

'Not for several months.'

'He asked after you. Did you ever find out what he was doing with Thelma?'

'No.' Magnus had seen Tryggvi Thór and Thelma having lunch together, shortly after they had both denied knowing each other. And after Tryggvi Thór had been attacked. Twice. 'He said, if I didn't shut up asking him about it, he'd throw me out.'

'Well, he can't do that any more, can he?'

'No,' Magnus admitted. But Ingileif was right – he should stay in touch with the old man. 'I'll give him a call. Maybe you could come with me? He always liked you.'

'Maybe.' Ingileif's voice was cool. Maybe not.

Dinner was over, Magnus had done the washing up and Ási was in his bedroom, when she sat on the sofa and asked him to join her.

She took his hand, her face determined.

'Magnús. I'm going to ask you a question, and it's important you answer honestly.'

'OK,' he said.

'Are you Erla's father?'

He squeezed her hand. 'No,' he said simply, meeting her grey eyes.

Ingileif seemed to hesitate. He felt the pressure of her removing her hand, and then she squeezed it. 'OK,' she said. 'I believe you.'

'Thank you,' said Magnus. And he really meant it.

'I decided I was going to trust you and you were going to trust me, and I'm not going to give up on that. So I believe you. But you've got to admit that Erla and Ási do look similar?'

Magnus didn't answer.

'What about getting married?'

'Do you still want to do that?' Magnus blurted out.

'Oh, yes,' said Ingileif. 'Now more than ever. I don't mind telling you, I feel vulnerable. I'm trusting you totally when my head is telling me I shouldn't. But I'm overruling my head. I need you to trust me.'

'I *do* trust you.'

'Do you? That's not what you said yesterday.'

She was right, it wasn't. And yet.

'OK. I understand. Just give me some time to think about it. Not years, like I said yesterday. Days. OK?'

'OK,' Ingileif nodded.

Magnus admired her. She was taking a risk with him. And, given her track record, the whole commitment thing was a bigger deal for her than for many other people. He had no doubt of her sincerity.

But, as she said, Erla and Ási did look a lot alike. And there was a reason for that.

Magnus was worried about Vigdís. And he wanted to share that worry with Ingileif.

'You know I told you that Vigdís saw her mother hit someone in her car on Tuesday?'

'Yes?'

'He died.'

Ingileif gasped. 'Oh, no! Have they arrested Audur?'

'Vigdís hasn't told anyone what she saw. Apart from me.'

'Oh. That's not good.'

'No, it's not. I've told her to come clean. I've given her twenty-four hours to do it, or else I'll do it for her.'

'Do you think she will?"

'I hope so. I'm sure she will. She's a good cop.'

'What if she doesn't?'

Magnus shrugged. 'If she doesn't, I'll speak to the officer who took her statement.'

Ingileif looked at Magnus steadily. He knew what she was thinking. 'I have to, Ingileif! Once cops start covering for other cops then the whole thing becomes rotten. I saw it in Boston. I'm not going to be part of it here.'

'But it's her mother,' Ingileif said quietly. 'You can't expect her to testify against her mother.'

'I would,' said Magnus, anger tingeing his voice. From

nowhere he could feel the emotion bubbling up inside him. It was all he could do to restrain a sob.

'I know how you feel about your mother, Magnús, how angry you are with her,' Ingileif said gently.

Magnus *was* angry with his mother. While he was living it, his childhood hadn't made any sense. His first memories were of warmth and happiness in a tiny metal-clad house on the hill in Reykjavík with a little tree he could climb in the front yard. His mother going off to teach at the local secondary school. His father at the university. The family laughing together, all of them happy.

Then his father left them to go to a university in America. At first, Ollie, Magnus and their mother were supposed to follow him, but then they didn't. The two brothers moved up to their grandparents' farm in Snaefellsnes where life became a nightmare. Their grandfather was cruel to the point of sadism; their grandmother looked the other way. Their mother became sleepy or silly and did nothing to protect the boys from her own father. There were times of manic laughter, but mostly life was miserable.

Then there was a car accident and she died. And Magnus's father came back from America to rescue him.

As a teenager, Magnus had begun to make sense of all this. His mother was an alcoholic. She had chased her husband away. Then she had got drunk and driven into a rock, probably intentionally. She probably intended to abandon her sons to her own parents.

She had hurt Magnus badly, and ruined Ollie's life. Magnus couldn't forgive her.

He had subsequently discovered, after his return to Iceland as a cop, that there were other reasons why drink had got the better of her. Magnus's father had started an affair with her best friend. But even with that knowledge, he couldn't forgive her.

He hadn't been able to explain this to anyone. Except Ingileif. Ingileif had understood.

'This isn't about your mother, is it?' Ingileif said.

'No. And I know it's dreadful for Vigdís. But this woman should be locked up. What about the guy she hit? What about the guy's family? What about the next guy she hits, next week or next month? What about them?'

'I'm not saying Vigdís shouldn't say what she saw,' Ingileif said.

'So what are you saying?'

'I'm saying that if Vigdís hasn't changed her story by this time tomorrow, talk to me before you do anything.'

'All right,' Magnus said. 'All right. I'll talk to you.'

His phone beeped. Ingileif rolled her eyes.

But the text wasn't from the station. It was from Louisa.

I have some important information about Pybus-Smith's death. Can I come and see you at 10 a.m. tomorrow? Louisa.

TWENTY-TWO

Louisa didn't show at 10 a.m. Vigdís was writing up the assault in Kópavogur. They had one poor description of the thug to go on. Big, light brown hair, small beard, blurred ink on his neck.

No sign of Louisa at ten-thirty.

Magnus texted her. No response.

By eleven, Magnus was worried. A foreigner missing an appointment with the police should be no big deal. Perhaps she had decided to drop the whole thing? Perhaps whatever she thought was important hadn't seemed so important in the light of day?

But he had seen enough of Louisa to know she would take an appointment with the police seriously. If she had changed her mind or if something else had come up, she would have told him. Louisa was the kind of woman who didn't miss appointments.

He had a bad feeling about this.

'I'm going to Louisa's Airbnb,' he told Vigdís.

'Really?'

'I don't like it.'

'Suit yourself,' said Vigdís, going back to her computer.

Magnus drove the short distance. He rang the bell to Louisa's flat. No answer. He tried again. Nothing.

The entrance to the flat was through a white door just beside the clothes-store front. There was a key box with a combination – no doubt tenants were given the code when they arrived at the start of their stay.

Magnus called Vigdís. 'She's not there,' he said.

'Maybe she's gone for a coffee.'

'Without contacting me? Can you get hold of Airbnb and tell them to find someone to let me in? Say we are worried about their tenant's safety.'

'Seriously?'

'Seriously. She had important information for me today. I'm worried. I hope I'm wrong.'

'Fair enough,' said Vigdís.

Magnus grabbed a cup of coffee at a café across the road. Five minutes later, he received a text: *The owner will be round in ten minutes.*

The owner was a man in his thirties wearing a suit but no tie – a banker or businessman who bought properties to rent out on Airbnb on the side.

Magnus introduced himself. 'Your tenant is Louisa Sugarman, right?' he asked.

'That's right. She's taken the place for two weeks. She said she was visiting friends in Iceland when I exchanged emails with her. Your colleague said you were worried about her?'

'I am. Do you mind if we go in and check on her?'

'Sure.' He pulled out some keys and unlocked the door of the building. Louisa's flat was on the first floor.

Magnus stopped the man as he was about to unlock the

door and gave him a pair of disposable gloves, putting some gloves on himself.

The man raised his eyebrows, but put them on, turned the key and made way for Magnus to enter.

Louisa Sugarman was lying on the floor of the living room, face up, her blood staining the fine weathered floorboards.

TWENTY-THREE

October 1940

Neville Pybus-Smith was worried.

He scanned the typed sheet in front of him. It was a translation by his interpreter Gunnar of the lead article in the latest issue of *Thjóðviljinn* – the small but nasty left-wing newspaper.

The article was encouraging Icelanders who were working for the British to go on strike.

Neville was becoming increasingly worried about the communists. They were trying to turn a war between Britain and Germany – democracy and Fascism – into a class struggle between the workers and the capitalists. The British were the capitalists and the Icelandic labourers were the workers. In this view of the world, British working-class soldiers should side with the Icelandic labourers rather than with their own army.

Neville was certain that it wasn't just theories of class consciousness that drew *Thjóðviljinn* to this conclusion; the fact that the Soviet Union and Germany had signed the Molotov–Ribbentrop Pact the year before had a lot to do with it. And the money he believed the newspaper received from Russia.

Dockers had just gone on strike and Dagsbrún, a trade union, had been handing out pamphlets to English soldiers urging them in English: *Don't be a scab! Don't take the job of the Icelandic working man!*

The irony was that times had never been better for the Icelandic working man. His labour was needed by the British for unloading at the docks and for the construction of an airfield on the edge of Reykjavík and a naval base at Hvalfjördur. Demand for cod from Icelandic trawlers in Britain had skyrocketed as many of the Hull and Grimsby fishermen had been recruited for the Royal Navy and the merchant marine. There was good money to be made.

Neville was a banker. He understood economics. In such a tight labour market, the power was with the workers. They could ask for high wages and probably get them. He could live with that.

What he couldn't live with was communist propaganda corrupting the British soldier and turning him against his own country.

Neville needed help. A British officer who spoke, or at least understood, Icelandic.

Lieutenant Marks.

Marks would be ideal. Neville liked what he had seen of the man. As well as his language skills, he had the intelligence for the work and he related well to Icelanders.

One Icelander in particular. Neville's mind drifted in a direction which had become familiar over the previous couple of weeks. He felt a stiffening in his trousers, also a familiar feeling.

Kristín.

He couldn't get her out of his mind. He could recall her smile, her flashing eyes, her red hair, so clearly. During their conversation in the Hotel Borg, he had aroused her interest, he was sure of it. And he was pretty certain it wasn't just because he had power over her brother.

Neville knew he had a way with women. He had good looks, charm, and he was an English gentleman. There were precious few of those in Iceland. Certainly, there were plenty of British officers in the country, but most of those were oiks – lingerie salesmen or bookkeepers who had scraped a commission while the army was desperate.

His erection wouldn't go away.

Neville had needs like any healthy man in his prime – probably more than most, he suspected. It had been six months since he had had sex. He had ceased having marital relations with his wife years before when Tabby was born, but there were always interesting and interested women to be found in London, mostly married to someone else. Failing that, there were the comforts of a little place he knew in Shepherd's Market.

There were good-looking women in Iceland, but there were also thousands of British men. Some had been lucky enough to snap up a girlfriend – Shaw from Divisional HQ, for example, had become very friendly with the daughter of the family with whom he was billeted. The family Neville was billeted with had three sons. Thanks partly to Neville's efforts, the Hotel Borg no longer allowed entry to other ranks, and there was dancing there in the evenings, yet there were still a dozen eager officers for every available woman.

Most of them were not available. '*Skilekkis*', they were called, after the Icelandic phrase '*Ég skil ekki*', meaning 'I don't understand'. It's what they claimed whenever soldiers tried to chat them up.

The answer to his problem must lie outside Reykjavík.

Specifically, the answer must lie on a farm on the shores of Hvalfjördur outside Reykjavík.

But Kristín was a *skilekki* – those were the words she had used when he had tried to talk to her that evening. And Neville had still picked up only a couple of phrases of Icelandic himself. He couldn't very well bring Marks along to translate for him.

Would it matter? Wouldn't a girl like Kristín be excited to meet a gentleman like Neville? Surely he must be more interesting to her than whatever oaf lived on the farm next door?

There was only one way to find out.

Tom rode his motorbike back to C Company HQ in Hvammsvík. He had spent the morning with Captain Chappell of the Royal Engineers and two representatives of the Icelanders working on the construction of the naval base.

Tom was impressed by Chappell and his RE colleagues. Hundreds of British soldiers and Icelandic labourers busied themselves around half-built concrete structures, with lorries, cranes and cement mixers clanking and grinding all around them. All those people, all that machinery, all that activity shattered the haunting beauty of the Whale Fjord as the war reached out its tentacles over the North Atlantic to spoil even this isolated corner of the world. Damp hill-sides and dark waters brooded their disapproval. Yet the steep mountainsides and the sandy brown fortress of rock that reared up above Hvammsvík seemed to offer the prospect of security and safety to the warships who would shelter here, twenty miles inland from the open sea.

It was the Royal Engineers who worked day and night coordinating everything and everyone. Despite the long hours, Chappell seemed to have bottomless reserves of energy and resourcefulness, and he somehow managed to communicate his enthusiasm to the soldiers and the labourers.

But the labourers wanted more money, and Chappell needed Tom's help to negotiate with them. The morning's discussions had gone well: Tom hoped that a strike would be avoided.

He had spotted Kristín's brother Siggi among a group of labourers having a fag break and had nodded to him, but Siggi had looked the other way. Fair enough. Tom could understand his reluctance to be associated with the occupiers.

As Tom dismounted from his motorcycle, a corporal approached him, saluted, and told him that Major Harris would like to see him in his Nissen hut. Tom noticed a powerful American car, a dark blue Ford, parked just outside. A whiff of sulphur leaking from some nearby crack in the ground tickled his nostrils.

He found his commanding officer finishing lunch with a man he recognized: Captain Pybus-Smith. They were both smoking cigars and a three-quarters-empty bottle of Johnnie Walker Black Label stood between them.

'Ah, Tom. Pull up a pew, old man. Can I pour you a drop? It's good stuff.'

'No, thank you, sir,' said Tom. Regular army officers liked to emphasize their professionalism when compared to territorials like himself. But he had come to realize that life for officers in the pre-war regular army had consisted of three hours' work in the morning, then a large alcohol-fuelled lunch and a nap in the afternoon. Some of them, including Major Harris, had found the habit difficult to break.

Tom hadn't the time. Perhaps he hadn't mastered the regular officers' skills in delegating.

Or perhaps he just wasn't lazy.

'Pybus-Smith here says he wants to borrow you again on a more formal basis.' The major was slurring his words. 'Says you did a damned fine job for him on the *Pestmomo*.'

'The *Esja*, sir. From Petsamo. In Finland.'

'Yes, that's right,' said Harris. 'Anyway, he'd like your help with the communists in Reykjavík. Stirring up trouble on the docks. I said you were helping out here with them.'

'I could use a man of your intelligence and language skills,' said Pybus-Smith with a friendly grin. 'Are you sure you won't take a drop?'

'No, thank you, sir,' said Tom. 'I think I'm pretty much fully employed at Tóftir. In fact, I need to get back there now.'

'Well, think it over, both of you,' said Pybus-Smith, refilling his glass, and the major's. 'But before you go, Marks, can you tell me where that man Marteinn Hálfdánsson lives? You know, that communist we interrogated from the *Esja*.'

Tom frowned. Did Pybus-Smith really want to see Hálfdánsson? Or did he want to see Hálfdánsdóttir?

He was drunk. And he looked . . . dangerous.

'He lives at Laxahóll. It's just a few miles beyond Tóftir. There's a turn-off to it just opposite an old farmhouse with a turf roof – it's signposted, I think. I can show you if you like. As I said, I'm heading back that direction.

'Don't worry, old man. I'll just look in on my way to Reykjavík. I've got my car. Laxa-hoddle, you say?'

'More or less. Is that your Ford outside?'

'Yes. Rather nice, isn't she? V-8 DeLuxe Tudor. Requisitioned it from a businessman in Reykjavík, who had imported it from America. Lovely to drive.'

'You don't have a driver?'

'Usually I do, but I thought I'd take her for a spin myself today.'

Pybus-Smith was much too drunk to get behind a wheel. 'I can drive you if you like,' Tom said. 'You'll need a translator.'

'I'll manage. Didn't you say you had things to do?'

'Are you sure?' said Tom.

'Quite sure,' said Pybus-Smith. With a grin.

It wasn't the grin of someone about to interview a communist farm worker in a language he didn't understand.

Reluctantly, Tom left the two officers to their whisky and rode his motorbike back along the edge of the fjord to his platoon at Tóftir.

TWENTY-FOUR

September 2023

Louisa Sugarman had been dead at least eight hours when her body was discovered just after eleven o'clock in the morning. She had texted Magnus at nine-thirty-two the previous evening. She was still wearing clothes – she hadn't changed into night things. Which meant she had probably been killed between nine-thirty-five and about midnight that evening.

She had been stabbed twice in the chest. There was no sign of the murder weapon. There was plenty of blood; some of it would probably have transferred on to the murderer. No sign of defensive injuries to the hands or arms.

No sign of a break-in either. It was possible that Louisa had known her killer and let him or her in, but on the other hand, the killer might simply have had a plausible story.

Her purse was still in her handbag, containing a full

complement of credit cards and some cash. No sign of a phone.

The flat above was rented out to tourists as well; a couple had gone out for the evening and returned at about eleven-thirty. They hadn't seen or heard anyone come in, or any commotion on the floor below, which suggested a two-hour window between nine-thirty-five and eleven-thirty for the murder.

There were plenty of Louisa's own fingerprints in the flat, as well as some of Magnus's and the woman who cleaned the place. There were also at least six separate unidentified fingerprints, probably from previous tourist occupants. Since the flat was cleaned between each visit, these were few and far between, and the technicians were working on isolating them. There didn't seem to be any fresh fingerprints on the most likely surfaces that a recent intruder might touch, such as doorknobs.

The most obvious line of inquiry was that Louisa had discovered something the previous day about Neville Pybus-Smith's death and that someone had wanted to prevent her from telling Magnus. Presumably, it was something Louisa hadn't known when she had spoken to Magnus earlier that afternoon.

Magnus had left the apartment at about three o'clock. So where had Louisa been between then and nine-thirty-two when she had sent the text to Magnus?

There were plenty of security cameras on Hverfisgata, although none that specifically covered the entrance to the flat. But police officers were checking them for signs of Louisa.

Her rental car was parked in a car park just a couple of blocks away on Saebraut, the road that ran along the bay.

More officers were checking whether she had driven it that afternoon and where.

Plenty to do.

After Magnus had set people to do it, he took Vigdís with him to go and see Gudni.

Magnus and Vigdís waited patiently while Gudni poured them both a cup of coffee. It seemed to be taking the old man forever.

'Now, how can I help you?' he asked eventually as he sank into his armchair and slurped from his own mug.

'We'd like to ask you some more questions about Louisa Sugarman.'

'Yes? I'm not sure there's much more I can add since I spoke to you yesterday.'

'Have you seen her since then? Has she been in contact with you?'

'No.' Gudni frowned. 'Did you tell her I saw her father kill my mother?'

Magnus nodded. 'Yesterday afternoon.'

'She can't have been happy to hear that.'

'She wasn't,' said Magnus. 'That's why I wondered whether she had been in touch.'

'Well, she hasn't. Not yet, at any rate. I suppose you did have to tell her?'

'We did. She had a right to know.'

Gudni shrugged. 'Perhaps. She might have been better off not knowing. That's why I didn't mention it when she came to see me.'

The unpleasant thought occurred to Magnus that Louisa Sugarman might still be alive if he had decided not to pass on Gudni's accusation to her.

'Gudni. Louisa was murdered last night.'

It seemed to take a few seconds for this news to sink in. If it was news.

Gudni frowned. 'Murdered? Do you know who did it?'

'Not yet,' said Magnus. 'But I'm sure we'll soon find out.'

'You think it has something to do with her father killing my mother?'

'Perhaps.'

'How?'

Magnus sighed. That was a good question. 'She sent me a text saying she had some new information for me and she wanted to see me this morning. She never got the chance.'

'I see.' Gudni shook his head. 'I'm sorry, I've no idea what that information was.'

'You told us yesterday that Louisa mentioned a Captain Neville Pybus-Smith?'

'Yes, she did. She seemed to think he had killed my mother. I didn't have the heart to tell her she was wrong.'

'Did she say anything about Pybus-Smith being murdered himself? In London in 1985?'

'No.' Gudni's eyes widened. 'No, she didn't.'

'That's funny. Because she said yesterday she'd told you.'

'Did she?' Gudni's gaze clouded. 'She might have done. I don't know. I wasn't really listening. I was thinking about what her father had done and whether I should tell her about it. What it would be like knowing you were the daughter of a murderer. Whether that was as bad as being the son of someone who was murdered.'

He shook his head. 'I shouldn't have worried about it. She found out from you anyway. And now she's dead.'

Magnus wondered if Gudni was needling him intentionally. If he was, it was working.

'Did you talk to your son Bjarni about any of this?' Vigdís asked.

'Oh, yes,' said Gudni. 'Once I had decided to tell you what really happened back in 1940, I asked him to take me to the police station. I wanted the moral support.'

'How much did you tell him about Louisa?'

'Just what I said to you.'

'And about Neville Pybus-Smith?'

This question caused Gudni to pause. 'I'm not sure,' he said eventually.

'How can you be not sure?' said Magnus.

Gudni shook his head. 'I'm not sure about a lot of things these days.'

'Where were you yesterday evening between nine-thirty and midnight?'

Gudni raised his eyebrows. 'Do you think I killed her?'

'Where were you?' Magnus repeated.

'Well, I started going to bed about nine. It takes a while to get myself organized these days. I probably turned the light off about ten.'

'Can anyone confirm that?'

Gudni chuckled. 'Hard as you might find it to believe this, I went to bed alone, inspector. Like I do every night. And the idea that I murdered anyone is absurd. I'm eighty-nine years of age. I don't have the strength. I don't have a gun. How was she killed anyway?'

'She was stabbed,' said Magnus.

Gudni shook his head. 'How exactly would I stab a strong and healthy woman like Louisa? I don't even know where she was killed. You guys haven't a clue.'

. . .

'Do you think he's acting or do you think he's genuinely confused?' Vigdís asked as they drove back to the station.

'I think he's as sharp as a tack, that one. He knew all about Pybus-Smith's murder.'

'But he seemed genuinely surprised by Louisa's death.'

'Maybe. Maybe not.'

'And he's right,' Vigdís said. 'I can't see him physically overcoming Louisa, even with a knife.'

'He could have caught her by surprise,' said Magnus. 'Look, we don't have any evidence yet that he killed her. But I'm damned sure he's hiding something. Let's get a warrant for his phone records and to search his apartment and examine his clothes. We also need to talk to his son. We should put in a formal request for the case file on Pybus-Smith's murder from London.'

'What about the journalist who broke the story? Amanda Wicker? We could try to track her down.'

'We could indeed.'

TWENTY-FIVE

'So, you want to speak to me about Neville Pybus-Smith's murder?'

Amanda Wicker's dark hair hung down beside a face scored with deep vertical lines. Her lips pointed downwards, giving the impression of a permanent scowl, but her brown eyes were lively. She was appearing by video link on Magnus's computer, his own image and that of Vigdís in small boxes on the right of the screen. Books were stuffed into the bookshelf behind the journalist higgledy-piggledy, suggesting more than just a backdrop for show.

'That's right,' said Magnus. 'We've read the articles you wrote in 1990.'

'And why would the Icelandic police possibly be interested in that?'

'We are investigating a homicide here. We're not sure, but there may be a link to Pybus-Smith's murder in 1985.'

'The mysterious Scandinavians?'

'Before we go any further, I'd like to keep this off the record.'

'Why should I talk to you off the record?'

Magnus had been expecting this. 'We've contacted the Metropolitan Police in London, but I'm not confident we will receive any help from them.'

'You can be confident you won't.'

'Quite. But if there is a link between that murder and the one here in Iceland, then it will prove that Joyce Morgan was innocent.'

'Which would be a great comfort to her,' said Amanda. 'I mean that sincerely. But I also mean that I would want to write about it.'

'OK,' said Magnus. 'Here's what I can do. If the two murders are linked, I'll give you a heads-up when we make an arrest. You'll get the press release at the same time the Icelandic media do. But you will be the only one who knows about the 1985 murder. What you do with the information will be up to you.'

Amanda Wicker was thinking, mulling over negotiating strategies.

'Amanda, I need your help. If my hunch is right, Joyce Morgan is innocent. You care about that: I know you do.'

'She was finally let out in 2007,' said Amanda. 'I never understood why she went down for murder and not manslaughter if it was a sex game gone wrong. The worst thing, the thing that really pains her, is that both her sons are now in prison. She's convinced that if she had been around when they were growing up, they wouldn't be in there now. She's probably right.'

Magnus understood her anger. Prison could run in families: he had seen it many times in Boston and often even in Iceland. And if it was a bent British cop who put the mother in prison, he bore the responsibility for the sons as well.

'So do we have a deal?' Magnus asked.

Amanda paused a moment before nodding. 'We do. What do you want to know?'

'Firstly, have you been contacted recently by a woman named Louisa Sugarman?'

Amanda shook her head. 'Never heard of her.'

'Are you sure?'

'Quite sure. Who is she?'

'She's the murder victim. She was killed some time last night here in Reykjavík. She said she was going to speak with you about Pybus-Smith's murder. I guess she never got the chance.'

'No, she didn't,' said Amanda, pausing to scribble down the name.

'What about those two Scandinavians? Can you tell me anything more about them than you put in the article?'

'I dug out my notes just now after I got your email asking to interview me. There was an older man and a younger man. The younger one was tall and blond. No real description of the older man, apart from he had grey hair.'

'And they were speaking Swedish?'

'Joyce had watched a lot of Swedish porn films in her sex work and she said they sounded a bit like the actors in one of those.'

'Could they have been speaking Icelandic?'

'Funnily enough, I wondered about that. I knew that Pybus-Smith had been stationed in Iceland during the war. But Joyce couldn't be sure what language it was. Is there an Icelandic connection?'

Amanda Wicker was an old-school journalist in her sixties. Magnus trusted her to stick to their agreement.

'There may have been. We think two young Icelanders were shot by a British officer in 1940.'

'Pybus-Smith?'

'Someone else. We think.' Magnus glanced at Vigdís, staring at her own computer at her desk opposite him. 'We don't know.'

'So, this would be some kind of revenge killing? That's a long time later, isn't it – 1940 to 1985? That's forty-five years.'

'That's true,' Magnus admitted. 'I was trying to put together a timeline from your article for the night of the murder.' He checked his notes. 'I couldn't see how it was possible for Joyce to have left the building at nine-forty-five having murdered Pybus-Smith when he made that phone call to the minicab firm at nine-forty-seven.'

'The police claimed that the witness who saw her leave at nine-forty-five was wrong.'

'But that still doesn't add up, unless the witness was wrong by at least half an hour.'

'No, it doesn't. And a young detective constable at the time admitted as much to me. He was the one who told me about the call to the minicab company and he corroborated Joyce's claims that she and other girls had provided sexual favours to the detective chief inspector in charge of the case. He was certain his bosses were out to get her – he heard them say as much. This was all off the record, of course: his career would have been over if they had found out he'd spoken to me. You see, I *knew* Joyce had been framed. That's why it was all so frustrating, and why I kept at it.'

'What happened to the detective constable?'

'Chief superintendent now. Still a good contact. Still a good copper. The chief inspector who fitted up Joyce Morgan took early retirement in the 1990s before he was forced out of the Met by another corruption investigation. Classic bent-cop move.'

In theory, the young detective constable should have

reported what he knew to his superiors rather than going to the press anonymously, but Magnus could understand how hard that would have been back in those days, how small the chances were that anything would result from it apart from the end of the constable's career. It would be hard even now, as Magnus well knew. He had first been transferred to Iceland to escape the consequences of reporting the tampering of evidence by bent cops in Boston to protect a local drug gang.

'Can I talk to this chief superintendent?'

'Definitely not.'

'What about the bent cop?'

'Not him either. But that's because he died ten years ago.'

On Magnus's computer screen Amanda frowned.

'What is it?' he asked.

'I've just remembered. You know Joyce specialized in S&M?'

'Yes.'

'We had an interesting conversation about it once. About why these men enjoyed it.'

'And?'

'She said there were a variety of reasons. For some of them, either being beaten or doing the beating at boarding school during adolescence inspired their fantasies. For one or two, it was something darker.'

'What do you mean?'

'Self-loathing. A desire to punish themselves. She had one client who had shot some German prisoners of war in Italy. That was why he wanted her to whip him.'

'And Pybus-Smith had something similar?'

'Joyce thought so, from what he said. He was never specific and she didn't want to ask. But yes, he believed he had done something very bad for which he should be punished.'

'Interesting.'

'Do you know what that might be?'

'Yes,' said Magnus. 'I think I do.'

'Did you understand all of that?' Magnus asked Vigdís as Amanda Wicker's image disappeared from the screen.

He was never sure how good Vigdís's English was. She refused to speak it but he knew she understood something, more than she let on.

'I got the gist of it,' Vigdís said. 'It makes me wonder whether Gudni was lying about seeing Louisa's father shooting his mother.'

'I wonder that too.'

'And what do you think his son Bjarni looked like in 1985?'

'I think he looked young and tall.' Magnus recalled the close-shaved stubble around Bjarni's scalp. 'With fair hair.'

'Which would imply that it wasn't Lieutenant Marks that Gudni saw shoot his mother.'

'It was Neville Pybus-Smith.'

TWENTY-SIX

Magnus and Vigdís entered the interview room, Vigdís with a folder under her arm containing evidence gathered during the search of Gudni's apartment in Grafarholt. The search was still continuing. Gudni had a lifetime of paper crammed into his small apartment and it was taking hours to go through it all. But his clothes were already being analysed for bloodstains.

Gudni looked up from his chair. In the station, he appeared even smaller and frailer than he had at home, his long unkempt white hair a straggly mess. But his eyes were bright, defiant.

'You again?' he said. 'Can we get on with this?'

Magnus and Vigdís sat down opposite him. The video-recording equipment was already on. Vigdís placed her folder in front of her: it contained a couple of items which Gudni might have difficulty explaining.

Magnus cleared his throat and formally identified himself and Vigdís. 'Gudni, I must inform you that we are now treating you as a suspect in the murder of Louisa

Sugarman. This means you have a right to a lawyer if you wish.'

'I don't need a lawyer. But I do want to talk to my son.'

'That won't be possible just yet. Your son is next door. We will interview him next.'

'Is he a suspect too?'

'He certainly is.'

Gudni snorted. 'Ridiculous. All right, what do you want to know?'

'Were you in London on the twelfth of March 1985?'

'How should I know?' said Gudni. 'I can't remember that far back.' He chuckled. 'I'm not sure what I was doing this time last week. But I'd say no. We were living in Kópavogur then.'

'Did you travel to London in 1985?'

'I said, I don't know.'

'Think.'

Gudni shrugged.

'Have you ever been to London at all?' Vigdís asked.

Gudni nodded. 'Yes. I've been a couple of times on short holidays with the family. But probably not in the mid-eighties. The kids were grown then. But I also went to see Spurs sometimes.'

'How often?'

'In those days, once every couple of years. It was expensive and my wife wasn't keen on me going away too often. After she died, I went more frequently. But it's even more expensive now.'

'Who did you go with?'

'Usually a friend from work. Bragi Örn. He's long dead now. Once or twice with my uncle and cousin.'

'Not with your son?'

'Bjarni? Again, once or twice. But he never really liked football.'

'Did you go to see Spurs in 1985?'

Gudni nodded. 'Eighty-four/eighty-five was a good season for Spurs. Came third in the league. I think that year I saw them play Ipswich Town. We lost three–two. Leworthy scored twice. I thought he was a good player, but he only stayed with us a few months. I wonder what happened to him?'

Didn't seem much wrong with Gudni's memory, Magnus thought. He knew dementia could strike randomly, destroying some memories and preserving others. But it seemed to him that Gudni's forgetfulness was far from random.

Vigdís produced a programme from the match, the words *Tottenham Hotspur* picked out in blue over a photograph of a man in a white shirt and black shorts leaping to head a ball. In smaller letters on the cover were the words *Saturday, 20 April 1985*. 'We found this in your flat.'

Gudni picked up the programme and leafed through it. 'It was always a shame to spend all that money and travel that distance to watch them lose.'

'Did you see any other matches that year?'

'Not that season,' said Gudni. 'I went to see them play Luton in eighty-six. Nil-all draw. Another waste of money.'

'So you didn't go in March eighty-five?'

'No. Have you found a programme?'

'We haven't,' said Vigdís. 'But you could have got rid of it.'

'Why would I do that?' said Gudni. 'I'd never throw away a programme.'

'To stop us finding it,' said Vigdís.

Gudni snorted.

'You told us you saw Lieutenant Tom Marks shoot your mother,' Magnus said.

'That's right.'

'But you didn't, did you?'

Gudni blinked. 'Yes, I did. I told you. That's something I *can* remember.'

'Then how do you explain this?'

Magnus nodded to Vigdís who extracted an airmail envelope from her folder. She passed it to Gudni.

It was addressed to him. It bore a stamp of Queen Elizabeth.

His shoulders slumped. 'I'd forgotten I still had that.'

'But you remember its contents?' Magnus asked.

Gudni extracted two sheets of thin airmail paper and scanned the black handwriting.

Meadow House School
Benningsby
Nr Skipton
North Yorks
England

8th February 1985

Dear Gudni,
I was so pleased to receive your letter! You were lucky to find me at the same address. I suppose you must have got it from those Christmas cards I sent your family after the war. This is my last year as headmaster here and I will be retiring in the summer. I am planning to buy a house somewhere

by the sea in the West Country; I will be sure to send you our new address when that happens.

I've enjoyed teaching, but I have hung on too long as it is. I will be seventy-one next month.

I visited Iceland a few years ago with my daughter. We went to Laxahóll, but your grandfather had sold the farm. I should have tracked you down then.

I'm so sorry you witnessed your mother being shot. That must have been truly dreadful for a six-year-old boy. I'm not surprised you didn't tell anyone at the time, especially if the man who shot her threatened you.

I do know who the British soldier with the little moustache was: Captain Neville Pybus-Smith. He was in charge of military intelligence in Iceland. He had met your mother a couple of times before, and I knew he was attracted to her.

I was convinced at the time that he killed your uncle and your mother and somehow disposed of their bodies. I have no direct evidence, but I remember the afternoon when they "disappeared" very well. Pybus-Smith was drunk, and he said he was going to interview your uncle at Laxahóll. I'm sure what he really wanted to do was see your mother who, as you know, was a very beautiful woman.

He subsequently claimed that he went straight on to Reykjavik and never stopped at the farm. Since he was in charge of the investigation into Kristín and Marteinn's disappearance from the British side, it was difficult for me to dispute this. I discussed my suspicions with my commanding officer who advised me to stay quiet.

I didn't. I confronted Pybus-Smith himself, but he denied ever having stopped at Laxahóll. He was adamant, and convincing, except I wasn't convinced. Everyone else was, though. I tried talking to a captain in the Military Police and finally the general staff officer at Divisional HQ, but no one wanted to know. The idea of a British officer being responsible for the deaths of two missing Icelanders did not appeal. If I had had hard evidence, their reaction might have been different, but I didn't have any real evidence at all.

I visited Laxahóll a few days after the disappearance, but only once. Your poor grandfather was in a daze of misery. Your uncle Siggi was angry at me and all the British. Only you were pleased to see me. We had a last kick around with the football I gave you, before your uncle chased me away.

I left Iceland with the 49th Division the following year when the Americans took over. Pybus-Smith stayed on as intelligence officer, before eventually handing over to an American. I believe he was sent back to England in disgrace after he tortured some Icelandic prisoners.

After the war, he had a classic career as one of 'the

great and the good', meaning he became a director of a number of companies including the merchant bank he worked for, and chair of a couple of government organizations. He was knighted four years ago, so he is now Sir Neville Pybus-Smith.

It makes me sick. I'm sure you have worked out by now that I was in love with your mother. I was devastated when she disappeared. I got married after the war – my wife died a few years ago – but I still think of your mother. Often.

And you too. I enjoyed kicking a football around with you. Do you still support Spurs? Can you do that from Iceland? I do, despite being surrounded by Leeds United fans. I coached the school's first eleven for as long as I decently could.

You also asked for the officer's address. I have done some digging and discovered he has two: one in Hampshire and one in London.

They are: Cherry Tree House, Chellingham, Andover, Hants and in London: Flat 12, Eton Court, Porlock Square, South Kensington.

Don't tell me why you want his address. But when you have time, tell me your own news.

Yours ever,
Tom Marks

Gudni pursed his lips and looked up from the letter to Magnus.

'It really doesn't sound to me as if the last time you saw Tom Marks he was waving a pistol at you and threatening you to keep quiet because he had just shot your mother.' Magnus peered at Gudni. 'Does it sound like that to you?'

'No.'

'So why did you lie to us?'

Gudni's eyes fell to the letter. He didn't reply.

'Was it because you knew that it was actually Pybus-Smith who had shot your mother but you wanted to put us off the scent? In case we realized it was you who killed him in London. For revenge.'

Gudni didn't move.

Magnus waited.

'I wish you hadn't told Louisa that her father shot my mother,' Gudni said at last.

'Because it wasn't true?'

'Because she died believing it was.'

'For what it's worth,' Magnus said, 'I don't think she did believe it.'

'That still leaves the question: why did you lie to us?' Vigdís said.

'We know you saw *someone* shoot your mother,' Magnus said. 'You knew she had been shot in the head, so you must have witnessed it yourself. Was it this British officer with the small moustache? Neville Pybus-Smith?'

Tears appeared in Gudni's eyes. He nodded. He looked up. The tears came fast, running along the crags and creases of his face. He made no attempt to stop them.

'Well?' Magnus said. 'Why didn't you want us to know that?'

No answer. The pain in Gudni's watery eyes tugged at

Magnus. But he knew he was getting somewhere. All he needed to do was push harder.

'You went to London in March 1985, didn't you? With your son, Bjarni? You went to Pybus-Smith's block of flats. You passed a black woman on your way in. And when he let you into his flat you strangled him. Was it you? Or was it Bjarni?'

Nothing.

'That black woman went to jail for twenty years, you know? For a crime she didn't commit. A crime *you* committed.'

Gudni slumped back in his chair and let his eyes drop.

'What about Louisa?' said Vigdís. 'How much of this had she discovered? What was she planning to tell us?'

Gudni muttered something inaudible.

'What was that?' said Magnus.

'I didn't kill Louisa,' he said, still not raising his eyes. 'And neither did Bjarni.'

TWENTY-SEVEN

Before interviewing Bjarni, Magnus caught up with his team. As usual in a murder investigation, the atmosphere was one of excitement and activity – Icelanders worked fast in a crisis. But as usual, Magnus was wary. Speed was important, but so was thoroughness. He would much rather his officers took an extra hour over a task than that they missed a clue or a connection.

Five hours after the discovery of Louisa's body, there was a lot to report, a lot still to investigate. There had been no obvious signs of blood on Gudni's clothes, but forensics were taking a closer look. No communications with Louisa on Gudni's phone or his computer, although he had spoken to his son Bjarni three times in the previous forty-eight hours, including just after Louisa came to see him.

Police in Britain had tracked down her two adult daughters but were still trying to find Louisa's husband, or rather ex-husband, Daniel Sugarman. They had been divorced ten years.

Nothing from the phone company yet about Louisa's phone. Magnus was hopeful that if her murderer had grabbed her phone and hadn't switched it off, then it might leave a trail and perhaps even point to his whereabouts. If he had had the sense to switch it off or take out the SIM, then that action would give an idea of the time of the attack.

CCTV at the car park on Saebraut showed Louisa leaving in her rental car at 4.45 p.m. the previous afternoon and returning at 8.15 p.m. Where did she go? Whom did she speak to? What information had they given her that she wanted to pass on to Magnus?

Two officers had been looking at footage from the CCTV up and down Hverfisgata. It was hard to be sure because it was dark and raining, but they hadn't spotted any images of a small, frail old man matching Gudni's description between 9.30 p.m. and midnight. Magnus asked them to check again for Bjarni, whose photograph had now been taken.

Forensics were still trying to untangle the various traces of fingerprints in Louisa's apartment. The most interesting was a print on her bag. It wasn't hers, and it hadn't matched anything in the LÖKE database. Her phone could well have been in that bag, so there was a good chance the print belonged to whoever had stabbed her and then taken her phone. Magnus asked them to check the sample against Bjarni's prints.

He set them all back to work and called the prosecutor to brief her on how the case was progressing and to ask her to arrange a warrant for Bjarni's phone and computer and his clothes. If Louisa hadn't been in touch with Gudni, maybe she had spoken to Bjarni.

Then he went outside the police station to talk to the gaggle of reporters and cameramen hanging around the entrance. He identified the victim as Louisa Sugarman, a British citizen, and asked any member of the public who had seen her between 3 p.m. and 9.30 p.m. the day before to come forward. He answered questions about suspects with an assurance that the investigation was progressing well. An officer handed out photographs of Louisa for the reporters.

Bjarni was not happy when Vigdís and Magnus entered the interview room.

'I've been here nearly two hours!' he said. 'They tell me I'm under arrest so I can't leave. That can't be right.'

'It is, Bjarni,' said Magnus, taking a seat opposite him. 'We can hold you for twenty-four hours, longer if a magistrate allows it. But you are entitled to a lawyer.'

Bjarni took a breath and glared at Magnus. 'You've made a mistake. I hope we can straighten everything out now and I can go. But, yes, if you try to hold me for twenty-four hours, I will want a lawyer.'

'Fair enough,' said Magnus. He quickly ran through the formalities to start the interview. 'We need to ask you about Louisa Sugarman,' he began.

'She's the Englishwoman I'm supposed to have killed?'

'She was murdered yesterday and that's what we are investigating,' Magnus confirmed. 'And you are a suspect. Have you ever met her?'

'No,' said Bjarni.

'What do you know about her?'

'Just what Dad told me yesterday. He called me after she came to see him in Grafarholt. He said she was the daughter of a British officer who had been in Iceland during the war. This man had been in love with Dad's mother – that's my grandmother.'

'Kristín Hálfdánsdóttir?'

'That's right. Anyway, Louisa had got the wrong end of the stick about who had killed Kristín and Marteinn. She had the wrong guy. It was actually Louisa's father who had shot them. And Dad wanted me to bring him here so that he could tell you. He was really upset about it, understandably, as you saw.'

'Did you know that your father had seen who'd shot Kristín?'

'No, I had no idea until then. I knew my grandmother and her brother had disappeared during the war. I asked Dad about it a couple of times, but he always refused to talk about it. It was clearly painful – I mean Dad was just a little boy when it happened. I spoke to Uncle Siggi about it once – he was Dad's uncle, not mine. Kristín's younger brother. He said he was away from Laxahóll at the time, working for the British on the naval base, but he always believed she had been killed by the British. He never liked the British.'

'Siggi must be long dead by now?' said Magnus.

'Oh, yes. He died in about 2000. He was in his late seventies.'

'Can you tell me a little bit about him? I understand he ran off with a girl from the neighbouring farm, who I think we've met?'

'Yes, that's right. Frída. He was married at the time, to a woman called Sunna. My grandfather was very unhappy about it and kicked him out, so Siggi went to live at Selvík and ended up running the farm there. This was in the early sixties – Dad had left home by then. Siggi had helped bring up Dad after Kristín died, with Sunna. Dad kept in touch with him, despite my grandfather's disapproval, and so I saw him occasionally.'

'OK. You say you didn't know for sure that Kristín had been killed by a British officer until yesterday?'

'That's right.'

'Did your father say why he hadn't told anyone what he had seen until now?'

'Yes. You asked him, and I heard him answer you. It made perfect sense to me. You see, I knew his mother's disappearance cast a shadow over Dad's life. If he didn't want to dig up the past, that was his choice. His right. I wasn't going to do it for him.'

'You know he was lying to us?' Magnus said.

'About what?'

'About Lieutenant Marks killing Kristín and Marteinn.'

Bjarni frowned. 'Are you sure? My father is an honest man.'

'Turns out he isn't. He did see a British officer killing his mother, but it wasn't Lieutenant Marks. It was Captain Pybus-Smith. He admitted it just now.'

'Did he? Oh. And this is related to Louisa Sugarman's death somehow?'

'We believe it is.'

Bjarni paused. Thinking. 'How?'

'We were hoping you would tell us.'

Bjarni snorted. 'I have no idea what's going on. I do know my father didn't kill this Louisa woman.'

'What about you? Did you kill her?'

'No! Of course not. Why would I kill her?'

Magnus glanced at Vigdís.

'How old are you?' she asked.

'Sixty-two.'

'So, how old were you in 1985?'

'I was . . . twenty-four, I suppose.'

'And you had a full head of hair, then? Blond hair?'

'Yes. I didn't start going bald until my thirties. And, as you can see, what little hair I have left is still mostly blond.'

Bjarni touched the thin, closely cropped hairs edging his shiny scalp.

'Did you travel to London in March 1985?'

'No.'

'Are you sure? Because, you see, a tall young man with blond hair and speaking a Scandinavian language was seen entering the apartment building in which Sir Neville Pybus-Smith was murdered, along with an older grey-haired guy.'

'It wasn't me,' Bjarni said with confidence. 'I was in the States then, doing a master's degree. At Florida State University.'

'Have you ever been to London?'

'Yes, plenty of times. But not so much when I was in my twenties, and definitely not when I was in the States.'

'Did you ever go with your father?'

'We went a couple of times as a family when I was a kid. And I went once to see Spurs with him and Uncle Siggi. But I was younger then – about eighteen. And I never liked watching football, much to Dad's disappointment. So, no, I'm quite sure I didn't travel to London in March 1985, either by myself or with Dad.'

'All right,' said Magnus. 'What about last night? What were you doing after nine-thirty last night?'

'That's easy,' said Bjarni. 'I took some German clients out for dinner with a colleague of mine from work. We went to an Indian restaurant, Austur-Indíafélagid. I've found clients seem to like the concept of Indian food in Iceland. We finished about ten-thirty and I called cabs for everyone. I got home to Kópavogur about eleven, maybe eleven-fifteen.'

Vigdís glanced at Magnus. 'That restaurant is on Hverfisgata, isn't it?'

'Yes. So?'

'So Louisa Sugarman was found dead in her Airbnb which is also on Hverfisgata,' said Magnus. 'About a hundred metres from the restaurant.'

'Whoa!' said Bjarni, frowning. He shook his head. 'Look, that's just a coincidence. I got in a cab right at the restaurant. I can give you the number of the driver. And my colleague, María, took a different cab at about the same time. María called three taxis. We put the clients in the first one and then took the other two ourselves.'

'You said you called the cabs,' said Vigdís.

'I know. I misspoke. It was María.' For the first time, Bjarni looked worried. 'Here, I've got her number. And she'll have the number of the cab company.' He pulled out his phone and read out a number.

'And what about the German clients? Can you give me their names and where they are staying?'

'We don't need to involve them, do we? I'm hoping to get a big contract to supply their furniture to an office refurb in Vogar. It won't look good if they are contacted by the police about my involvement in a murder.'

Magnus raised his eyebrows. 'It won't look any better if you are locked up in Hólmsheidi, now, will it?'

'All right,' Bjarni said. 'But they flew back to Germany this morning. I can give you their names and numbers at their offices in Munich.'

There was a knock at the door, and a constable appeared with a note. Magnus scanned it.

Location signals show Louisa's phone moved from her apartment on Hverfisgata to shore of the bay on Saebraut. Went dead at 10.42 p.m. Probably thrown in the sea by murderer?

Magnus showed the note to Vigdís. 'Interesting, don't you think?'

Vigdís nodded.

Bjarni was watching in confusion, barely resisting the urge to ask what was in the note.

'Thank you, Bjarni, that's all for now,' said Magnus. 'You've given us some leads to check. And we will be going to your home to examine your clothes for blood. We've requested a warrant to look at your phone and your computer.'

'In the meantime, can I go?'

'No,' said Magnus, folding the note and putting it in his pocket. He checked his watch. 'You've done three hours. Twenty-one more to go. We will definitely have more questions for you.'

'I'll want a lawyer.'

'You'll need one.'

'What do you think?' said Vigdís as they returned to their desks. 'He was leaving a restaurant in Hverfisgata minutes before Louisa's phone was thrown into the bay. Can that just be a coincidence?'

'We'll soon find out,' said Magnus. 'In the meantime, get over to his house with a couple of officers and talk to his wife. The warrant for his clothes should have come through by now.'

'All right.'

'Oh, Vigdís?'

'Yes?'

'You know I gave you twenty-four hours? To correct your statement about your mother?'

'Yes?'

'Let's call it forty-eight, shall we?'

'Thanks,' said Vigdís. 'I'm not sure that will change anything. I haven't had a chance to think about it with everything that's going on.'

'I get that,' said Magnus. 'But you do have to think about it. And the quicker, the better. For you.'

Vigdís grunted.

'And there's something else.' Magnus winced, suddenly unsure of himself.

'What's that?'

'I think I'm going to have to tell Ingileif. About Erla.'

Vigdís scowled. 'You promised you wouldn't tell anyone.'

'I know. I'm sorry, Vigdís. I don't have a choice.'

TWENTY-EIGHT

Vigdís headed for home straight from Bjarni's house in Kópavogur. His wife had backed up his story: he had returned home at about eleven-fifteen – she wasn't sure of the exact time.

Could he have thrown the phone into the bay at ten-forty-two, run back to the restaurant and caught a taxi, getting to Kópavogur at eleven-fifteen? It would be tight, but it was just possible. Also, a wife's testimony in support of her husband was always suspect; she could just be lying.

There was no visible blood on Bjarni's clothes and they would be added to Gudni's in the forensic labs.

As Magnus had said, they would soon find out whether Bjarni and his father had killed Louisa.

Magnus.

It was good he had given her another twenty-four hours to make up her mind, but the truth was her mind was already made up.

She couldn't rat on her mother. She just couldn't. Magnus didn't understand that. She was pretty sure he was expecting her to do what he considered her duty, in which case he wouldn't have to report her. In a way, that was a sign of his confidence in her. It was also a sign he didn't understand her.

His telling Ingileif about Erla was less of a worry – for Vigdís, at any rate. It's true she had made him swear never to tell anyone at all. But Vigdís trusted Ingileif to keep quiet. It was much more of a problem for Magnus.

What about her mother? Audur probably didn't even know yet that the jogger had died. Vigdís hadn't heard anything about it on the news, although it might well have been reported.

Audur also didn't know or didn't care that Vigdís was about to blow up her career for her.

Anger boiled inside Vigdís. It was all very well feeling irritation at Magnus. The person she should really be angry with was her own mother.

She was driving along the main road approaching Hafnarfjördur and the turn-off for home. She decided to drive on.

To Keflavík.

Audur seemed sober as she opened the door to her daughter. But then Audur always seemed sober. She was good at that.

'Vigdís! This is a surprise.'

Audur led Vigdís into the living room. The TV was on – Audur flicked it off with the remote.

'I saw your friend Magnús on the news,' she said. 'The murdered Englishwoman in Hverfisgata. Have you been working on that case?'

'I have,' said Vigdís, flopping on to the sofa.

'Have you found who did it?'

'We've got a couple of suspects in custody. We'll know soon enough.'

'What's wrong?' Audur was looking closely at her daughter.

Vigdís leaned forward and looked her mother in the eye. 'You know that jogger you hit? He died.'

Audur winced. 'I know. That was on the news too.'

'His name was Markús Hauksson. He was twenty-six. He had a girlfriend. A mother and a father. Friends. A long life ahead of him.'

'It's awful,' said Audur. 'A terrible accident.'

'Accident?' Vigdís muttered.

'This doesn't make you change your mind, does it?' Audur said. 'You're not going to change your story?'

Vigdís took a deep breath. 'No,' she said.

'Oh, thank you, Vigdís!' Audur threw herself on the sofa beside her daughter and wrapped her arms around her.

Vigdís stiffened.

'You have no idea how grateful I am to you,' Audur went on. 'I couldn't bear going to jail again. I just couldn't bear it! And I won't drink any more, I promise. I swear to you I won't. Not even one glass!'

Vigdís didn't respond.

Audur let her go. Her delicate, pointed chin wavered. 'I went to my AA meeting last night. It helped. They are all behind me.'

'Magnús knows,' said Vigdís. 'I told him. Before I heard the guy was dead.'

'Oh. Is he going to say anything?'

'He says he will. Unless I say something first.'

'But you won't, will you, love?'

Vigdís shook her head. 'I should, Mum. But I can't. But that means that when Magnús tells our boss that I have given a false witness statement, I'll be in big trouble. I'll lose my job. My career will be over.'

Audur sat back and frowned. Then she smiled tentatively. 'But Magnús wouldn't do that to you, would he? You've been working together for years. He's your biggest fan. And you've always said he's a decent man.'

'He is.'

'No,' said Audur. 'We just need to brazen it out. Call his bluff. When it comes to it, I'm sure he won't shop you.'

'I think he will.'

'But you're not certain?'

'I'm not absolutely certain, no. But Magnús has a thing about cops bending the rules to look after each other. He almost got killed in Boston when he exposed his partner there for tampering with evidence. The penalty for exposing me would be much less.'

'But you're not just cops. You're friends.' Audur reached over to Vigdís's hand, but she withdrew it. 'Sometimes you've just got to take a risk, love. Trust in people's better natures.'

'Like mine?' said Vigdís. She felt the anger rising. Take advantage of people's better natures, more like.

'Yes. And Magnús's.'

'Mum. Unless you do something, I am going to lose my job. Magnús will tell Thelma what I have done. You will be arrested and go to jail anyway.'

'No, you're not listening, Vigdís! That's not going to happen. Trust me.'

'It is. And it's down to you.' Vigdís felt an urge to scream at her mother, but she controlled it. 'I've done my best to look after you for years and years. But now it's your turn to look after me.'

'What do you mean?'

'Turn yourself in. It's the only way.'

'Turn myself in?' Audur shook her head. She was appalled by the idea.

'You were drunk when you hit that poor man. You did kill him.'

'I know, but I've told you, it won't happen again.' Audur's bottom lip wobbled. 'I couldn't stand any more time in prison, Vigdís. You've no idea what it's like.'

'I'm a police officer, Mum, I know what it's like. It's my job to send people to prison. People who deserve it.'

'But I don't deserve it! It was an accident.'

'Mum. I'm asking you to do this for me. It's your choice.'

For a moment, Vigdís thought Audur was about to agree. Then she shook her head. 'Magnús won't do that to you. And if he does, he's no kind of friend. I'm *not* going to jail!'

TWENTY-NINE

Ingileif was already waiting for Magnus, sitting on a low wall outside the Höfdi House, a small white mansion that stood beside the bay. It was eight-thirty and Magnus had driven the short distance from police headquarters.

It was a fine, clear night, cool, but not cold. A half-moon illuminated the broad shoulders of Esja on the other side of the fjord. The dim shapes of ducks floated quietly in the gently lapping water. Lights of small craft glimmered in the bay.

'I heard you on the radio,' she said. 'Any luck catching the murderer?'

'I think so. We'll find out tomorrow.'

'Why drag me here?'

Magnus sat down next to her. 'You know why. This is where we first met.'

The Höfdi House was a solid white wooden building that had been lifted out of a bourgeois northern European suburb where it would have blended in nicely, and dumped in a treeless settlement built of corrugated metal and concrete, where it became the grandest place in town. As such it had famously played host to Reagan and Gorbachev in the 1980s.

'Where we second met,' said Ingileif. 'We first met in my gallery when you interviewed me.'

'You know what I mean.' After that first interview, fourteen years ago, just after Magnus had arrived as a detective in Iceland, Ingileif had called him and asked him to meet her right there, at the Höfdi House. She had given him vital information relating to the murder of a professor he was investigating.

More importantly for both of them, it was the beginning of something. The beginning of what was not yet, even now, completely clear.

'Perhaps I do.'

'I have two things to talk to you about.'

'You sound very serious.'

'Perhaps I am.'

'What things?'

Magnus took a deep breath. 'I need to tell you about Erla.'

'Oh,' said Ingileif. 'You do.' Magnus could hear the nervousness in her words.

'You're right, Erla looks a lot like Ási.'

'I knew it!' said Ingileif, her body stiffening, bitterness flooding her voice.

'Wait a moment,' said Magnus. 'Hear me out.'

Ingileif didn't reply. But she waited.

'They look similar because they're cousins.'

'Cousins?' Ingileif frowned. 'What does that mean, Magnús? How can they be cousins?'

Magnus waited. He wanted Ingileif to answer her own question.

The Höfdi House was floodlit, and Magnus could see

Ingileif's expression quite clearly in the reflection from its white walls.

Her face lightened for a moment in understanding and then darkened.

'You're telling me that the father is Ollie? Your brother?'

Magnus nodded.

'And you expect me to believe that?'

'Yes,' said Magnus. 'You remember how he came over here in the summer of 2021? How Vigdís and I went out with him and his friends?'

'Yes, of course I do. That's when I thought you and Vigdís slept together. When Erla was conceived.'

'She was conceived that night. But it was Ollie, not me, who slept with Vigdís.'

'Why would Vigdís sleep with your brother? He's a scumbag.'

'I'm not entirely sure. I wondered the same myself. I asked her, eventually. She said she was drunk. He was drunk. He's a good-looking scumbag, which I suppose is true. But most importantly, he wasn't going to be hanging around Iceland; he would be gone and out of her life in the morning.'

'She intended to get pregnant?'

'I don't know. I haven't asked her. Maybe.'

'Does Ollie know?'

'No. And Vigdís is hoping he'll never find out. I only discovered it six months ago when I noticed how similar Erla and Ási were. I did the maths and realized she was conceived when Ollie was in Iceland. I was pretty drunk myself that night, but I remembered that when we all broke up at the end of the evening I kind of left Ollie and Vigdís together. I asked her whether they'd slept together and eventually she admitted it. She made me promise I wouldn't tell anyone, including you.'

Ingileif shook her head. 'I can't believe it.'

Magnus took her hand and squeezed it. 'Please believe it.'

'Why didn't you tell me before?'

'Vigdís swore me to secrecy. I keep my word.'

'But you knew how upset I was. How upset I am.'

'I know. That's why I'm telling you now. I warned her I would.'

'What did she say?'

'I think she's more worried about what she's going to do about her mother at the moment.'

Magnus could see the glimmer of a tear in Ingileif's eyes. 'I'm afraid to believe you, Magnús.'

'What do you mean?'

'I mean, if you are lying to me now, I'd feel such a fool.'

'I'm not lying.'

'It's kind of obvious that you slept with Vigdís. That Erla is your daughter. It's not obvious that Vigdís slept with Ollie.'

'Isn't it? Because that's what happened.'

'God,' said Ingileif. 'Who knew this monogamy would be so hard?'

'It works for me,' said Magnus.

'I guess it works for me too,' said Ingileif.

'Do you believe me?'

Ingileif looked out over sparkles of moonlight on the dark bay. Magnus waited, his heart pounding.

In the end, she nodded. 'Yes, Magnús. Yes, I believe you.'

Magnus exhaled. 'Good,' he said. 'In that case, there's something else I want to talk to you about.'

'Oh God, Magnús. I hope it's not as difficult as that was.'

'So do I.' Magnus smiled. 'Will you marry me?'

THIRTY

Magnus was in a good mood when he drove into work the next morning.

Ingileif had said yes. They had managed to get a table at Grillmarkadurinn, one of the best and most expensive restaurants in town, and they had had a wonderful evening. They knew, now that they had both finally made the decision, that it was the right one.

Strangely, it had been Ingileif's doubts about him that had convinced Magnus that they should get married. Sure, given Ingileif's track record with other men, it was a risk. But Ingileif had demonstrated that she was willing to take a risk herself, that she was willing to trust him even when the evidence suggested she should not.

If she was willing to take that risk, so should he be.

Having taken it, Magnus found himself suddenly, euphorically, happy.

Ingileif started talking about the wedding. It was going to be big – no surprise there. It was also going to be in a church – a bit more of a surprise. Magnus managed to steer Ingileif away from the tiny chapel at Bjarnarhöfn, the farm on the Snaefellsnes peninsula where he had grown up, which had too many painful memories. But Ingileif quickly fixed on the 'Black Church', a slightly bigger building near the Hótel Búdir on the other side of the peninsula, with a wonderful view over lava fields to the majestic Snaefell-sjökull volcano.

It was everyone's favourite wedding location, but Ingileif was sure she could swing it. Of course she could.

Magnus was also feeling confident that he had the murderers of Sir Neville Pybus-Smith and Louisa Sugarman in custody. There were some legitimate questions still to be answered, but he hoped those would all be sorted out that morning.

They weren't.

There was a buzz of excitement at the meeting Magnus called at eight-thirty, but as various officers reported the results of their different lines of inquiry, the mood deflated.

The fingerprints on Louisa's bag did not belong to Bjarni. Gudni's old cancelled passport from the 1980s had been found during the search of his flat. Stamps showed that he had arrived in the United Kingdom on 19 April 1985, but he had not entered the country at all in March. María, Bjarni's colleague, had seen Bjarni get into a taxi at about 10.30 p.m. at the Indian restaurant. The taxi driver was certain that he had picked up Bjarni from the steps of the restaurant at ten-thirty-four and that at ten-forty-two Bjarni was in his cab, not tossing a phone into the sea. He had records from an app to confirm precise timings.

Magnus was disappointed, but not downcast. He knew from experience the danger of becoming too wedded to a theory, of seeking out evidence which backed up that theory and ignoring anything that disproved it. They had had a hypothesis, it had turned out it was wrong, it was good they knew that now. Time to find a new theory.

'All right. We'll let Gudni and Bjarni go; we can always pull them back in if anything new turns up, but I'm not optimistic. Now it's even more necessary to find out what Louisa had discovered that she wanted to tell me. We need to track her movements, find out where she drove off to. She used a small local rental company – no GPS tracker, so they don't know where her car went. Someone must have seen her. Cameras will have captured her vehicle. Perhaps she bought petrol?

'Róbert?' Magnus asked one of his detectives. 'Get on to her family in England and check if Louisa mentioned anything about her trip to Iceland and her suspicions about Neville's murder. Especially if she phoned them or sent them a message in the twenty-four hours before she died.'

Vigdís's mind drifted as she listened to Magnus. She had registered that Gudni and Bjarni were off the hook and so they were back to square one, or perhaps square one-and-a-half. But she had been up half the night stewing. Her brain was tired, and it kept returning to her mother.

She had gone to bed sure that she would keep quiet and fairly sure that Magnus wouldn't. So her career would be over. This would be her last case. She guessed she would be suspended immediately, probably within minutes of Magnus telling whomever he decided to tell.

It made her immensely sad. She was a good detective. She enjoyed her work, even if she was occasionally irritated by internal politics and the interminable paperwork, or computerwork as it now was. She liked Magnus and her other colleagues. She didn't like Thelma, her boss, but then bosses came and bosses went.

That's who she was, who she had been her whole adult life. A police officer. A detective. She couldn't imagine doing anything else, being anything else.

Tears came, running down her cheek on to her pillow.

What would she do next? She had rent to pay, food to buy, for Erla as well as herself.

She had no idea.

But she knew she couldn't shop her own mother.

She had woken up shortly after 2 a.m. Wasn't there anything she could do?

No.

If only her mother would listen to her, listen properly. It wasn't as if sacrificing Vigdís's career would do her mother any good. She'd still wind up in jail once Magnus had reported her. Why couldn't she see that?

It was thanks to Audur that Vigdís had a career in the police in the first place. It had been hard growing up black in Iceland. There had been some overtly cruel racism, but most of it was just unthinking: Icelanders were unused to black people. Vigdís could deal with the individual slights, but they built up over a lifetime, a steadily increasing load that never went away.

Vigdís had been strong enough to bear that load, thanks to her mother. Audur was Vigdís's fiercest supporter, willing to go into battle anywhere at any time for her daughter.

When Vigdís had talked to a police recruiter about a job in the force and the man had laughed, telling her that the idea of a black policewoman wasn't conceivable in Iceland, Audur had been angry. Her anger turned into incandescent rage when she saw Snorri Gudmundsson, the head of the

Reykjavík Metropolitan Police, on television talking about how they needed police officers from minorities. She stormed into police headquarters first thing the next morning and demanded to see him. She was turned away.

But then she wrote a letter – this was back in the days when people still wrote letters. Two days later she received a phone call inviting her to come into headquarters and meet Snorri to discuss her daughter. Snorri listened and encouraged Vigdís to apply to the police.

So Audur had got her into the police force and now she was going to get her out.

Vigdís knew her mother. She was grasping at straws, and the one straw left was that Magnus wouldn't actually report her, or rather report Vigdís.

Was she right? Was there any way Vigdís could persuade Magnus not to talk?

No. Pleading wouldn't help. Pointing out the consequences for her if he spoke up wouldn't change his mind; he was already well aware of them. Vigdís didn't doubt Magnus's affection and loyalty towards her. That was the problem. She knew he believed that when cops put their loyalty to other cops above the law, everything fell apart. It was partly because the results would be so consequential that Magnus would think it important to do what he considered the right thing.

So Vigdís's career was over and her mother was going to jail.

In which case, why not just turn Audur in herself? Then only one of them would suffer.

Sending her own mother to jail was unthinkable, but it was also logical.

Vigdís just couldn't do it. How could she live with herself afterwards? For Magnus, loyalty to justice beat everything else. For Vigdís, it was loyalty to family, even if, apart from Erla, her only family was her drunken mother, who seemed happy to put her own survival before her daughter's.

But keeping quiet, sacrificing both of them, didn't make sense.

At 5.09 a.m., according to the numbers on her phone by the side of her bed, Vigdís decided she would call Lúdvík and tell him what she had seen. She would still be in trouble – she was convinced Thelma had it in for her – but her career would probably survive. She knew Magnus would be right behind her.

But she would feel terrible. How could she live with herself?

She'd just have to. She'd call Lúdvík as soon as possible that morning.

As soon as possible meant when the meeting was over.

She could see Magnus was wrapping up, so she slipped out and left the building by the back entrance into the car park, crammed with an assortment of police vehicles. She moved away from the door and leaned against the black railings. She selected Lúdvík's number in Hafnarfjördur.

She heard his voice as he picked up. 'Hi, Vigdís.'

She couldn't do it. She *just* couldn't do it. She couldn't tell this policeman that her mother had run over someone and killed them when drunk.

'Vigdís? Is that you?'

She shook herself. 'Yes, Lúdvík. Sorry, it's me, I was distracted. I wondered how your investigation was going? Into the hit and run. Any progress?'

'Nothing so far, beyond the silver car. Why, have you got something for me?'

'No, I was just curious. Sorry, I've got to go.'

She winced as she put down the phone. That was it. It was all over.

Magnus returned to his desk. There was plenty to do, but he needed a few minutes to think. Thinking was underestimated.

Vigdís showed up and sat silently at his desk, waiting. It was good to have Vigdís there – she could help him do the thinking. She had done that many times before.

She looked a bit down – her mother, no doubt. They could talk about that later.

'We can assume it wasn't Gudni and Bjarni who killed Louisa and Neville Pybus-Smith,' Magnus said. 'Gudni wasn't in London in March 1985, and although Bjarni could perhaps have flown there from university in Florida, it's unlikely.'

'Bjarni definitely didn't throw Louisa's phone into the bay at ten-forty-two,' said Vigdís. 'It's very hard to believe that Gudni stabbed Louisa and then ditched the phone in the sea. He's just too old and frail. And I never understood why he would wait forty-five years to get his revenge. Why not do something earlier?'

'All right. If it wasn't them, who was it?'

They sat in silence for a few more moments.

'Someone else who didn't want Louisa to tell you what she'd found out,' said Vigdís. 'But what was that?'

'Probably – and I say probably, not certainly – something about Neville Pybus-Smith's murder.'

'If those two Scandinavians Joyce Morgan saw entering Pybus-Smith's building were not Gudni and Bjarni, then who were they?'

Magnus grabbed a sheet of paper and a pen and began drawing.

'What are you doing?'

'Drawing a family tree.'

A minute later, Magnus looked over the diagram he had sketched and showed it to Vigdís.

At the top was Hálfdán, the farmer at Laxahóll. Beneath him were his children, Kristín, Marteinn and Siggi. Beneath Kristín was Gudni and beneath Gudni, Bjarni.

Next to Siggi Magnus had scribbled two names: on one side Sunna and on the other Frída of Selvík. Beneath Siggi and Frída was Jón.

It was possible that there were other cousins or offspring who hadn't been mentioned to Magnus yet, but for now, this list would do.

He thought a moment.

'We need an older man in 1985.' He circled a name. 'And we need a younger one.' He circled another one. 'What do you think?'

Vigdís squinted at the diagram thoughtfully. Then she perked up. 'I think you've got it! Let's go.'

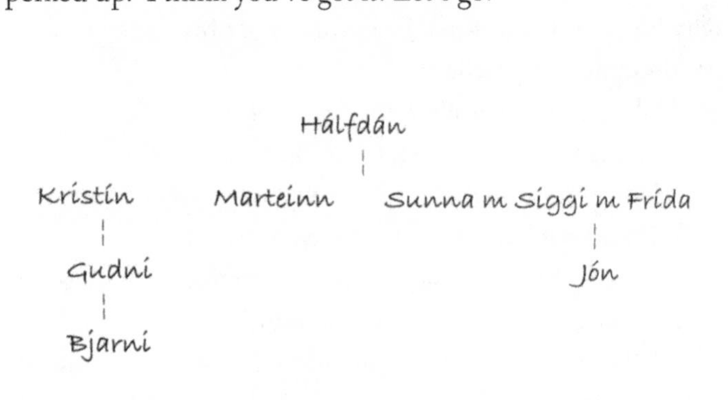

THIRTY-ONE

October 1940

Neville stood and stared at the two bodies splayed on the ground in the farmyard, just in front of the barn.

He looked at the gun hanging limply from his right hand.

Gunpowder tickled his nostrils.

What had he done?

His thoughts were whirling, leaping, lurching around his alcohol-disrupted brain. He had to steady them. Focus. Work out what the hell to do next.

What had he done?

He had driven up to the farm full of whisky-enhanced confidence. He was lucky that Kristín was there. He was even luckier that she was alone, except for her small son, whom she had quickly shooed up to his room to play.

She was polite and welcoming and seemed untroubled by their inability to speak the same language. She had given him a cup of coffee and a slice of cake. The enforced silence had been a little awkward, but he had turned on his full charm and managed a couple of witty mimes. She had laughed and looked away demurely.

He couldn't believe his luck. This was not a situation that was going to repeat itself – alone with a beautiful girl who clearly liked him.

But it was difficult to do anything in the house with the kid upstairs.

What about one of the barns outside? Neville had had a thing about barns ever since a tumble with a farmer's daughter at his cousin's stables in the country when he was eighteen. That had taken place in a tall shed with hay bales stacked fifteen feet high. These were squat buildings with thick low walls of stone and a turf roof of growing green grass. Cosy.

How to get Kristín out there?

He had an idea.

He got up to leave, and led her outside to where his motor car was waiting. Then he mimed looking and walking around the farm.

The girl smiled but shook her head.

Neville made for the barns. He could hear and smell the sheep in the larger of the two turf buildings – the hay was presumably kept in the smaller one right next to it.

This was the moment. If she stayed where she was, it would indicate that she didn't want to do anything with him. But if she followed? If she followed, her meaning would be clear.

He reached the smaller of the two barns and opened the door.

He turned. She was following him! She was protesting something in Icelandic, but he knew what she really meant. He knew what she wanted.

He entered the barn. The ceiling was low and the only light came from the open door. The floor was bare earth. The barn was piled to the roof with hay. The interior was warm, sweet-smelling and slightly dusty. It immediately brought back memories of that other girl, the chubby farm girl, what was her name?

With his brain so fuzzy, Neville couldn't remember.

Didn't matter.

He moved over towards the hay and turned around.

Kristín was standing in the doorway. She said something and pointed back towards his car. She looked nervous – that was understandable. He grinned. She was in for some fun.

He moved towards her.

She took a step back.

He grabbed her arm.

He wasn't sure exactly what had happened next. He could remember the feelings that swirled around his intoxicated brain. Excitement. Euphoria. Lust. Then, as she resisted him, from somewhere deep inside, rage. Rage that like so many of the Icelanders he came across, she was obstructing him. Saying no – even he knew what *nei* meant. *Skilekki* be damned.

He knew he should stop; he needed to continue.

She screamed.

Did she mean that? What did she mean by that scream?

He didn't know, and he didn't care.

'Stop!' A male voice. Loud. Urgent. And in English.

He heard the word, but he ignored it.

Then there was a crash.

He looked up and saw her brother, that ratty little man, Marteinn, grasping a shotgun just outside the entrance to the barn, its barrel pointing upwards. He had fired into the air.

'Stop! I said stop!'

Neville climbed to his feet. His trousers, together with his holster, seemed to have fallen to his ankles, so he bent down to pick them up, and buckled his Sam Browne belt. Kristín was sobbing on the ground next to him.

This looked bad. However much Kristín had led him on, Neville knew this looked bad. Nothing had happened, though.

He could talk his way out of this.

He staggered past Marteinn into the farmyard and took a couple of deep breaths. His instinct was to get in the car and drive away.

Nothing had happened.

Yet it had. Marteinn would talk. To the Icelandic police, to the British military police, to the Icelandic authorities.

The British would have to take his allegations seriously. It wasn't just Neville's word against Marteinn's. There were two of them.

This would be hard to hush up.

Marteinn had one arm around his sister and the other was gripping his shotgun, double-barrelled with one cartridge still unfired. He was holding it in his left hand. In an odd moment of clarity, Neville remembered that Marteinn had used his right hand to pull the trigger for his first shot in the air.

Neville still had his sidearm in its holster.

He knew he was drunk. He would have to be careful, deliberate, if he wasn't to miss, even at this close range.

He stopped. Focused. Pulled out his pistol and pointed it at the Icelander.

As Marteinn let go of Kristín and passed the shotgun

from his left to his right hand, Neville pulled his own trigger. The bullet hit Marteinn in the chest. Marteinn dropped his weapon, and a second later he slumped to the ground.

Kristín looked at her brother in horror. Then she glared at Neville, fury and hatred in her eyes.

She launched herself towards him.

She was perhaps ten yards away. Enough time for Neville to raise the pistol again.

It swayed upwards in his unsteady hand as he pulled the trigger.

He hit her in the forehead and she fell like a stone.

Now what?

Christ knew.

He bent over the two bodies. Kristín was dead, the top of her head a bloody mess. His bullet had hit Marteinn in the heart; Neville watched as life ebbed from the man's blue eyes.

Had he really just killed two people? One of them the woman he had been fantasizing about for the last couple of weeks? The woman with whom he believed himself to be in love?

He had.

He felt numb. He felt as if he was about to throw up.

Don't throw up. Mustn't throw up. Mustn't leave a pile of vomit for people to find.

Think!

He needed a story. An explanation. For the farmer, when he came back. For the Icelandic police. He was a British officer, so they should believe him. But he needed to give them something to believe.

A story.

What story?

He could explain that it was all a misunderstanding, that Kristín had led him to the barn, that Marteinn had just got the wrong end of the stick, that Marteinn had been about to shoot him and that he had shot Marteinn first in self-defence.

And Kristín? Why had he shot Kristín?

Because he had had no choice. Because he had had no time to think. Because he had known she would testify that he had tried to force himself on her and had shot her brother.

That wouldn't work.

What if he said Marteinn had attacked him? That Marteinn was a communist spy who had been cornered?

And Kristín? She had attacked him too.

He would tie himself in knots trying to explain that one. The military police would see right through it.

All right. How about if he said he had never even been to Laxahóll? He was pretty sure no one had seen him driving up the track to the farm. That sounded right.

Then what about the bodies? Had some other unknown person arrived and shot them? Bloody Lieutenant Marks would testify that Neville was intending to visit the farm, as would Major Harris. And the bullets in the bodies came from a British officer's revolver. *His* revolver.

He had to move those bodies. Hide them somewhere, perhaps in the fjord. Except that would mean driving out on to the main road along the shore where he could be seen. What about that hollow he had seen driving up to Laxahóll? Then he would say he had never been to the farm at all.

As a plan, it was far from perfect, but it was the best he could think of. And he had to do *something*. He couldn't just stand there staring until the farmer arrived.

He felt a raindrop fall on his face, and then another. That was good, it would help hide any blood marks on the ground. Somewhere behind the rain clouds the sun was slipping below the horizon. The countryside was enveloped in a murky gloom. It would be dark very soon.

How to move the bodies?

Then he had a thought.

The boy! The damned boy!

He looked upwards at the farmhouse. He thought he saw a small head in one of the upstairs windows. Then it was gone.

He would have to deal with the damned boy.

An hour later, he climbed into the Ford, started up the engine, turned on the headlamps and windscreen wipers and drove slowly down the lane through the darkness to the main road along the fjord.

He had been lucky. He had found some sacking in the barn and had wrapped the two bodies in it. He had crammed them into the rear of the Ford, with the shotgun, and driven to the hollow he had spotted before.

No one had passed him along the track.

He had scouted out the hollow and found a crevasse just big enough to stuff the bodies into. There were plenty of loose stones and boulders around, and he had been able to cover the cleft in the rock completely. He decided to get rid of the shotgun later.

As he approached the end of the track to the junction with the main road, he turned off his glimmering headlights. Through the dark and the rain, he could just make out the shape of the old turf-covered farm on the shore of the fjord.

Yellow light from its windows. The inhabitants might hear his car, but they wouldn't see it.

He turned left and headed back to Reykjavík.

How had it happened? He still couldn't quite believe he had killed two people. It was self-defence: Marteinn had been just about to shoot him. Then he had had to kill Kristín; he had had no choice.

He knew he should have shot the boy. He just couldn't bring himself to do it. He had scared the living daylights out of him, though, threatened to come back and shoot him as well if he breathed a word to anyone. He just had to hope that that would be enough.

He should have shot him.

He swerved as he took a bend too fast. He slowed down. He was still drunk.

His luck would have to hold if he was going to get away with it.

There would be a search. The local police would be alerted. Neville would have to make sure he inserted himself as their point of contact. As head of military intelligence on the island, that should not be difficult. He would play up Marteinn's communist leanings.

When Lieutenant Marks found out that Kristín and her brother were missing, he would no doubt ask difficult questions, questions which Neville would answer with simple denials. He had driven straight back to Reykjavík from Hvammsvík. He never stopped at Laxahóll.

It would be difficult for Marks to get around Neville. He would have to persuade Neville's superiors at Divisional HQ to investigate him. That would be the last thing they would want to do. A British officer killing two Icelandic citizens would be a disaster for relations with the government. Even a hint of suspicion would be damaging.

No. Unless Marks had incontrovertible proof that Neville was involved, Divisional HQ would look firmly the other way.

As he stared grimly through the wipers at the road ahead, Neville thought he might just get away with it. As long as the kid stayed quiet. And the bodies weren't found.

He gripped the steering wheel tightly.

With luck, he might avoid justice. But he couldn't avoid himself.

He would always know that he had shot two people in cold blood. The hollow pain in the pit of his stomach was never going to go away.

He was a murderer and he always would be. For the rest of his life.

He pulled to the side of the road, the dark waters of Hvalfjördur dimly visible through the rain, leaned his head on the steering wheel and wept.

THIRTY-TWO

September 2023

Magnus and Vigdís drove east out of town and then north along the N1 Ring Road. As they were passing the turnoff to Thingvellir, Magnus's phone rang.

It was Líney, one of the uniformed sergeants on the team.

'What have you got?'

'Louisa used her credit card to buy petrol at the Olís petrol station in Grundarhverfi at five-twenty-two p.m.'

'That's just before the Hvalfjördur tunnel, right?'

'That's right.'

'Have you checked the tunnel cameras?'

There were cameras at the exit of the Hvalfjördur tunnel where the Ring Road headed north towards Borgarnes.

'Nothing.'

'So she turned off the Ring Road before the tunnel?'

'She must have.'

'Thanks, Líney.' The phone went dead.

Magnus turned to Vigdís and grinned. 'Looks like we're on the right track.'

Vigdís smiled weakly. 'It does.'

Magnus was acutely aware of the difference in mood between himself and Vigdís. It must be her mother. That would be a difficult conversation, but not for now.

Magnus decided to keep his news about Ingileif to himself; somehow flaunting his own happiness at that moment seemed wrong.

They reached the tunnel and turned right just before it. In a few minutes, they were following along the edge of Hvalfjördur. The ugly blue pipes of the aluminium smelter blighted the far shore; chunky grey clouds rolled around the steep hillsides on either side of the plant. A ray of yellow light beamed down at an angle onto the fjord's deep waters, turning grey into a ruffled circle of gold.

Vigdís's phone rang.

She answered. 'Hi, Lúdvík.'

Magnus flicked his eyes from the road to check Vigdís's expression. It was hard to read. Shocked? Surprised?

Lúdvík was doing all the talking, with Vigdís grunting in acknowledgement.

'Thanks for letting me know, Lúdvík,' she said eventually, hanging up.

She stared out of the car window at the fjord; Magnus couldn't see her expression. Then she turned towards him and a smile crept across her face.

'What is it?'

'That was Lúdvík. It's Mum. She just turned herself in at the police station. She admitted it was her who ran over the jogger.'

Magnus grinned. 'At last! Lúdvík doesn't know you saw her, does he?'

'I think he has probably guessed,' said Vigdís. 'But he's not going to say anything, I'm sure. He made a point of telling me he wouldn't need to look for any more witnesses now.'

'I always liked that guy. Did you talk your mother into it?'

'I tried. I thought I'd failed to get through. I was up all night stewing about it. As was she, it seems.'

'She did the right thing in the end.'

'You're not going to say anything now, are you?' said Vigdís, aware that she had still broken the law by giving a false witness statement.

'No,' said Magnus, smiling. 'Not even I am that much of a hard-arse.' He felt a surge of relief – he would have followed through on his threat to report Vigdís and that would have destroyed her career. He was profoundly grateful he hadn't had to do that. 'It's good news, Vigdís.'

'She's going to jail, though.'

Magnus thought Audur deserved what was coming to her; it was Vigdís who was the one who was suffering unjustifiably. And the poor guy whom Audur had killed. But he decided now wasn't the right time to tell Vigdís that.

'Right.' They were approaching Selvík and the turnoff to Laxahóll. 'Time to concentrate. We have a murder to solve.'

'Two murders,' Vigdís corrected him.

'Plus the two in 1940,' Magnus said. 'That makes four.'

Magnus scanned the fjord as he waited for the door to the farmhouse to be answered. Two grey sausages of seal sunned themselves on a rock only a few metres out from the shore, watching him and Vigdís, weighing up whether to slip into the sea or just to stay put. A small boat drifted far out in the water, within it a figure hunched over a fishing rod. A pair of ravens, perching on nearby fence posts, watched him.

Eventually, Frída opened the door, dressed in a skirt and a green lopi sweater. She smiled in an anxious greeting when she saw who it was.

'Hello, Frída. Can we speak to Jón?'

'He's out there, fishing.' She pointed to the man in the boat. She checked her watch. 'But he said he'd be back about now. I'm sure he won't be long. Come in and have a cup of coffee.'

Magnus and Vigdís sat at the table in the kitchen, familiar from their last visit only four days before. They waited as Frída fussed over a thermos of coffee and placed two slices of soda cake on plates in front of them.

'Is this about the murder of that poor Englishwoman I saw on the news last night?' Frída asked as she sat down opposite them with her own cup.

'Yes, it is,' said Magnus. 'Did she visit you on Thursday?'

The old woman sipped her coffee thoughtfully. Magnus and Vigdís waited.

She seemed to come to a decision. 'Yes, she did. Late afternoon.'

'About what time?' Magnus asked as Vigdís pulled out her notebook.

'I'm not sure, I didn't check the time. I'd say about six? It was still light; I was getting supper ready.'

'What did she want to talk to you about?'

'Her father. I told you she had visited us here a few

years ago. Her father was stationed here in the war and knew Kristín, the girl you found.'

'Yes. We know.'

'She spoke in English, mostly to Jón. My English isn't very good, but I got an idea of what she was saying.'

'And what was that?'

'She was very upset. Apparently, Gudni – you know who I mean?'

Magnus nodded.

'Well, Gudni had told you people that he had seen his mother and uncle being shot at Laxahóll when he was a little boy, and it was Louisa's father who had shot them. Louisa was certain this couldn't be true. She was desperate to prove that it wasn't him, it was another British officer called Neville something-or-other. She asked Jón if he knew anything that would prove her father was innocent.'

'And what did Jón say?'

'Jón said he didn't know anything.'

The woman frowned into her coffee.

Vigdís leaned forward; she had picked up on something. 'And what did you say, Frída?'

Frída looked up from her coffee directly at Vigdís, as if grateful she had been asked the question.

'I said I knew Neville had killed Kristín and Marteinn. I knew it wasn't her father.'

'And how do you know that?' Magnus asked quietly.

'My husband Siggi told me years ago. Gudni had told him. In secret – Gudni had never told the police what really happened. They were both adults, Gudni was visiting us here at the farm and he and Siggi stayed up late drinking. Since he was a kid, Gudni had been scared that Neville might come back and kill him if he found out he had told anyone.'

'When was this?' Vigdís asked.

'Sometime in the 1980s.'

'Why didn't you mention this to us?' Magnus asked.

'It's Gudni's secret, not mine. And at the time it didn't seem relevant.'

'Whereas it does now?'

Frída looked straight at Magnus. Her bright blue eyes showed the wisdom of the old. 'It was for Louisa. It seemed very relevant.'

'And to your son?' Vigdís asked.

Frída hesitated. 'He didn't think it was relevant,' she said eventually. 'Louisa said she would tell the police – you, presumably. I said that was fine. I assume she never got the chance?'

'No,' said Magnus.

Frída considered his answer and nodded.

'What did Jón think about her going to the police?' Vigdís asked.

'He didn't think it was necessary.'

'I see,' said Magnus. 'What time did Louisa leave?'

'I don't know. She was with us about an hour, maybe a little less.'

'And Jón? Did he stay at the farm all evening?'

'No,' Frída replied, weighing her words. 'He said he had to go into Reykjavík to get a part for his tractor.'

'At night?'

'He said he needed to use it first thing in the morning.'

'And what time was this?'

'I don't know. After supper.'

'When did he get back here?'

Frída shrugged. 'I was in bed.'

'What time do you go to bed?'

'About half past ten.'

So Jón could have been beside the bay at Saebraut in Reykjavík at 10.42 p.m. on Thursday evening when Louisa's phone went dead.

Magnus looked out of the kitchen window to the fjord. The boat was chugging towards the shore.

'Did Siggi ever travel to London with Jón?'

'We went together once, just Siggi and me. But with Jón?'

Magnus nodded.

Once again, Frída seemed to weigh her words carefully. 'Yes, they did go once. In the 1980s. To see a football match. Gudni is an avid Spurs fan, and he passed that on to Siggi and Jón, although they were nowhere near as keen as him.'

'Which year was that?'

Frída shook her head. 'I don't know. Mid-eighties sometime?'

Magnus and Vigdís sat in silence, processing the implications of what the old woman had just said.

'Wait a moment,' Frída said. 'I think I know where the programme for the match is. Jón kept it.'

She shuffled out of the room. Vigdís glanced at Magnus. 'Do you think she knows what she's doing?'

Magnus nodded. 'I think she does.' Out of the window, he saw the large figure of Jón drive the boat up to a dock and tie it up. He hoped Frída would hurry up.

She returned to the kitchen carrying a small booklet, which she handed to Magnus. On the cover, four men in white grinned as they lifted their arms in triumph. Tottenham Hotspur was playing Manchester United. Along a sidebar, a date was inscribed in small white letters.

Saturday, 12 March 1985.

The day Sir Neville Pybus-Smith was murdered.

THIRTY-THREE

Jón burst into the room carrying a blood-stained blue cooler. 'Two cod and a wolf fish,' he said.

Then he saw the two detectives. His eyes dropped to the programme in Magnus's hands.

'What are they doing here?'

'They've come to ask us about Louisa, love,' Frída said.

'Oh.' Jón frowned. 'I hope you waited for me before you spoke to them.'

'I answered their questions,' Frída said quietly.

The frown deepened. Jón put down his cooler, poured himself a cup of coffee and joined them around the kitchen table.

He glanced again at the programme, seemed about to say something, and then kept quiet.

'What were you doing in London on the twelfth of March 1985?' Magnus asked.

Jón took in a deep breath. 'Watching a football match with my dad,' he said. 'That one.'

'What else were you doing?'

He shook his head. 'Nothing. We stayed at a small hotel and came back to Iceland the following evening.'

'I see,' said Magnus. 'Last Thursday evening you drove into Reykjavík just a few hours after Louisa Sugarman visited you here. What were you doing then?'

'I needed to pick up a part for the tractor.'

'Which shop was open that late?'

Jón shifted uncomfortably in his chair.

Magnus stared at Jón. He was waiting for Jón to fill the silence, but it was Frída who spoke; her quavering voice had a hard edge.

'Jón. Tell them, love. Tell them what you and Siggi did in London.'

Jón turned to his mother. 'You know?'

'When Louisa told us that that Neville man had been murdered in the 1980s, I knew. Everything slotted into place. I remembered Siggi behaving very strangely when you came back from London. He was never really the same man after that. Now I know why.'

Jón glanced from his mother to Magnus and Vigdís. 'I don't know what she's talking about,' he said.

'I understand Neville's death,' Frída said. 'What he did to your grandmother was evil. But Louisa?' Tears welled up in the old woman's eyes. 'How could you do that to Louisa? She was only trying to get justice for her own father. And for the poor woman who was convicted of the murder.'

'Mum!' Anger flared in Jón's eyes. 'How can you say that? Do you know what you're doing?'

Frída's bottom lip trembled; the struggle of her own anger and sadness ravaged her face. A tear rolled down her cheek. 'How could you do that, Jón? How could you kill her?'

'This is bullshit!' Jón pushed back his chair and got to

his feet. Magnus tensed, ready to pounce if he made a run for it, or if he attacked his own mother. The big farmer fought to control his anger and then moved to the window, staring out at the fjord, his face hidden from the detectives.

'We know you killed Neville Pybus-Smith,' Magnus said quietly. 'And we know you killed Louisa.'

Magnus, Vigdís and the old woman waited for Jón to decide what to say.

He turned around to face them. 'I didn't know Dad was going to kill the Englishman,' he said eventually, so quietly that Magnus could barely hear him. 'I didn't even know he existed until after the match. Dad said we were going to visit someone: the British officer who had killed his brother and sister during the war.

'I knew about their disappearance, of course. It was a family legend, whispered about over the years. But until then, I had no idea they had been killed. Dad said my cousin Gudni had seen it happen when he was a little boy. Seen this British officer Neville Pybus-Smith shoot them both. Gudni kept quiet about it, but eventually he told Dad. Dad said we were just going to talk to this man, and that he had brought me along because I spoke English. I was twenty at the time.

'So, we went to this fancy apartment block in Kensington. Eton Court, it was called. We were going to ring the bell when a black lady came out of the building and let us in. We went up to Neville's floor and knocked on his door.

'He wasn't expecting us, and he wasn't pleased to see us, but Dad pushed past him into the flat. Then Dad made him sit down and I had to translate as Dad told him how he knew Neville had killed Kristín and Marteinn.

'Neville denied it and said that if we didn't leave his apartment immediately, he would call the police.'

Jón swallowed. 'Then Dad went for him. I wasn't expecting that at all, but he grabbed Neville by the neck and started squeezing. Neville was an old man, in his seventies, and although Dad wasn't very big, he was very strong. But Neville wriggled free and scrambled over to a desk. He opened a drawer and pulled out a gun.

'Dad was about to go for him, but stopped. Neville told him to back away – I was still translating. There was something about Neville's eyes, some kind of decision he had made. I knew he was going to shoot Dad. So I picked up a lamp and swung it, hitting Neville on the head.

'It was a good blow. Neville was out cold. Then Dad jumped on him and grabbed his neck again.'

'What did you do?' Magnus said.

'I just watched him. I hadn't realized until that moment that Dad had planned to kill Neville all along. But that's what he did. Right in front of my eyes.'

'Then what did you do?'

'We left. I thought to wipe down anything we had touched, and I grabbed the gun. Then we took the Underground back to our hotel and went back to Iceland the next day. I threw the gun away in a canal near the hotel.

'We both thought we would be caught. I was furious with Dad: he had suckered me into helping him. I'm sure that Neville deserved to die, but it wasn't up to us to kill him! I was only twenty and my father had made me a murderer. I found it hard to forgive him for that. I never did forgive him.' His mouth set in a grim scowl. 'Never.'

'Things were different between you after that trip,' said Frída. 'I remember. And I never understood why.'

'That was why. But it would all have rested there. Dad died more than twenty years ago. And then Gerdur decided to have her fun.' Jón's voice was bitter.

'What do you mean?' asked Magnus.

'That earthquake. Spitting out those remains for the stupid tourists to discover. You know, at first I really thought that skull belonged to her.'

'Jón, Gerdur died three hundred years ago,' said Frída. 'There's nothing left of her.'

Her son scowled.

'What happened when Louisa came here on Thursday?' Magnus asked.

'She was upset that Gudni had told you her father had shot Kristín and Marteinn. She didn't believe it was true and asked us whether we knew anything that would help her prove it. I said no.' He threw a glance of frustration at Frída. 'My mother said yes. She said Dad had told her that Gudni said it was another British officer who had killed them. I didn't know he had done that, that she knew.'

'What was Louisa's reaction?'

'She was relieved. Then she asked us whether we knew Neville had been murdered in 1985. We both said no – I think Mum genuinely didn't know anything about it. She certainly looked surprised.'

Frída nodded. 'That was the first I had heard of it.'

'But I don't think Louisa believed that I didn't know. I said Neville deserved it if he had killed my uncle and aunt. That was a mistake: Louisa immediately became suspicious. She told us about the black woman who had let us into the building and how she had been convicted for the murder and spent years in prison.

'She said she was going to the police to tell them that Gudni had lied to them about who shot Kristín and Marteinn. I decided against asking her not to do that – I thought it would just make me look guilty. But after she left, I realized that I had to persuade her to stay quiet somehow.

The more I thought about it, the more I felt I had a good chance: she clearly believed Neville was an evil man. He deserved to die. And even if she didn't approve of us killing Neville, it was nearly forty years ago and surely she could turn a blind eye?

'So I drove into Reykjavík. She had given us her address there and phone number – it was an apartment in Hverfisgata.'

Jón paused. Magnus, Vigdís and Frída waited.

'At first, she seemed sympathetic. She knew her father hated Neville and loved Kristín. She seemed to agree Neville needed to be punished for killing Kristín. But she thought murder was murder. The real problem was the black prostitute who had gone to jail for a crime she didn't commit.' Jón looked down. 'Then I lost my temper. I said what did it matter, she was only a whore. Louisa didn't like that. I knew I'd blown it.'

Jón stopped.

'And then?' Magnus said.

'Then I stabbed her.' Jón took a deep breath. 'I knew I could never persuade her. She said she was going to talk to you the next morning about Neville's death and I knew you'd figure out who had killed him. So I stabbed her. I wiped down her room and left. I threw her mobile phone into the sea – I thought it might have evidence on it – and came back here.'

'What did you stab her with?' Magnus asked quietly.

'A knife. I threw that in the sea too.'

'And where did you get the knife?'

'I brought it with me. It's one of the ones I use to gut fish.'

'Why?'

'In case.'

'In case what?'

Jón looked up at Magnus, but he didn't answer.

Premeditated, Magnus thought.

He had heard enough. The rest could be explained in the interview room at the station with a lawyer present. 'Jón Sigurdsson, I'm arresting you for the murder of Louisa Sugarman.'

He nodded to Vigdís, who took out a pair of handcuffs and snapped them on to his wrists.

As they were leading Jón to the car, Frída touched Magnus's arm. There were tears in her old eyes. Her wrinkled face seemed to crumple in on itself. She seemed devastated by the enormity of what she had done, but underneath her anguish, there was steel in the old woman.

'I had to tell you,' she said. 'I know he's my son, and I don't care about that horrible soldier. But he shouldn't have killed the poor woman! I had to tell you.'

Magnus watched as Vigdís pushed Jón into the back seat of Magnus's car.

'I can imagine how difficult that was for you,' he said. 'But you did the right thing.' He smiled with sympathy. 'I am sorry.'

Frída turned and hurried back into the warm farmhouse.

Had she done the right thing? Magnus had meant what he said when he had agreed with her. But he knew very well what Vigdís's opinion would be.

The truth was, he didn't know.

THIRTY-FOUR

Magnus and Vigdís transferred Jón to a police car which had met them on the main road into Reykjavík, and turned up the hill to Grafarholt. There would be plenty of time to question Jón more closely at the station, but Magnus wanted to have a word with Gudni first.

Vigdís's worried expression had returned; she was obviously thinking about her mother.

'You know Ingileif and I have decided to get married?' Magnus said. 'Properly. In a church.'

'Really?' Vigdís's face lit up with a genuine smile of pleasure. 'Congratulations! I didn't think Ingileif would go in for that sort of thing with you.'

'Neither did I. But she was the one who wanted to do it.'

Vigdís shook her head. 'And I thought she had good taste. Isn't that her job? To have good taste?'

'She almost didn't,' said Magnus. 'She thought I was Erla's father. That's why I had to tell her about you and Ollie.'

'Really? She really thought you and I had . . .'

'Really.'

'Yuck.'

'Yuck?'

Vigdís turned to Magnus. 'Yuck.'

They drove on in silence for a while, Vigdís staring out of the window at the new apartment buildings of Grafarholt. 'You know, I'm pleased we'll still be working together, Vigdís,' Magnus said.

Vigdís grunted and continued to look away. But Magnus could just make out the traces of a small smile on her lips.

Gudni was watching handball, not football, when he opened the door to them. 'You again,' he said grumpily. 'Do you want coffee?'

'No, thank you,' said Magnus. 'We'll only be a minute.'

Gudni led them into his living room and dropped into his armchair. Magnus and Vigdís perched on the sofa.

'We've just arrested Jón.'

'What for?'

'For the murder of Louisa Sugarman.'

Gudni nodded. 'Anything else?'

'We know that he and his father Siggi killed Neville Pybus-Smith in London in 1985. It's likely that the British authorities will want to talk to him about that. But it's not our jurisdiction. Louisa Sugarman's death is.'

'Stupid boy,' said Gudni. 'He shouldn't have done it.'

'No, he shouldn't.'

'I guessed it must have been him.'

'But you didn't know?'

'I didn't want to know.'

'That's why you lied about seeing Tom Marks kill your mother?'

Gudni nodded. 'I wanted to protect Jón: I hoped you would stop looking at Neville and the 1985 murder. Are you arresting me?'

'Not yet. You did try to obstruct our inquiry, but it will be up to the prosecutor whether you are charged for it. If Jón pleads guilty she might not charge you, given your age. I don't know – we'll see. We'll bring you into the station tomorrow for a statement. You should probably find yourself a lawyer.'

'I didn't know—'

Magnus held up his hand to stop Gudni. 'Best leave anything else to our interview tomorrow when you have a lawyer present.'

'Bjarni had nothing to do with any of it. You should know that.'

Magnus nodded. 'I hear you. We'll speak tomorrow. A police car will come here to fetch you in the morning.'

Gudni looked out of his window and watched the big red-haired detective and his black colleague leave the building and head towards their car.

He turned to the bookshelf where his mother's photograph album lay and pulled it out. Then he looked up at the piles of Tottenham Hotspur match programmes crammed into a higher shelf.

It took him five minutes to move the stepladder to the proper place, climb up and pull down the earliest programmes. Time was when he could reach that shelf without the ladder. He carried them over to his armchair and shuffled through them until he found the oldest: Spurs v Newcastle United, 10 November 1956. Spurs had won three–one and Gudni had been thrilled. His grandfather had paid for his ferry ticket to Scotland for his birthday and the visit to White Hart Lane had been the highlight of his first trip to Britain.

But that wasn't why he had picked out that particular programme.

Inside it was a blue airmail envelope addressed to him and postmarked nearly thirty years later. He had had the presence of mind to hide this one many years ago – he had simply forgotten about the other letter written a few weeks before it that the police had found.

He slumped into his armchair with the album and the programme, and slipped out a yellow newspaper cutting from the envelope. An obituary from *The Times*. A photograph of a self-satisfied Englishman with greying temples, a smug smile and a pencil-thin moustache was placed next to the headline: *Sir Neville Pybus-Smith CBE 24 October 1910–12 March 1985*.

A blue one-page note had come with it. Gudni cast his eyes over it.

Meadow House School
Benningsby
Nr Skipton
North Yorks
England

16th March 1985

Dear Gudni,

Well, what a coincidence! A month after I send you

Pybus-Smith's address, he is found dead in his flat in London. The newspapers are coy about the cause, although one of them, the News of the World, *hints at 'sex games'.*

I can't say I'm sorry. He was a truly evil man. At first, I assumed that it was you who travelled to London, but on reflection, I suspect that it was your uncle Siggi. He was an angry young man, and even though I didn't know him well, I imagine he is not the type to forget the death of his brother and sister.

Whichever one of you it was, I congratulate you. And rest assured, I give you my word I will say nothing to the police should they ever approach me, although I doubt they ever will.

I hope one day we will meet again in more peaceful circumstances.

Yours ever,
Tom

Despite Tom's hope, they never did meet again. Gudni had visited London many times over the years but had never made the diversion to Yorkshire, and, as far as he knew, Tom hadn't visited Iceland again.

The knowledge of the murder, and each man's ambivalent attitude towards it, had kept them apart.

It was clear that when Tom had written that letter, the murder investigation had not yet been announced in the press. Later, he must have read about the trial of Joyce Morgan and still kept quiet. Something had proved more powerful than testifying on behalf of an innocent woman. Loyalty to Gudni and Siggi? The desire for revenge? His own complicity with the murder?

When Siggi had asked Gudni to find out Neville's addresses in England, Siggi had assured him that he only intended to confront Kristín and Marteinn's killer. But actually, given how angry Siggi had been when Gudni had told him the year before how he had witnessed Neville shooting them in the farmyard at Laxahóll, Gudni wasn't surprised at what Siggi did. They never spoke about it; it was only from Tom's letter that Gudni even knew Neville had been murdered.

Like Tom, Gudni had no regrets about his part in what Siggi had done. Neville Pybus-Smith had deserved to die.

Siggi was stupid for involving his son, though.

Gudni understood why Tom's daughter, Louisa, had thought differently – an innocent woman had gone to jail for a crime she didn't commit, after all.

There was no excuse for Jón killing her. Idiot boy!

He opened the album and flicked through it again. He stared at the beautiful young woman standing next to a motorcycle, with a fjord in the background.

He let the programme, the letter and the cutting slide on to the floor next to his armchair.

He was tired. So tired.

It really was time to turn up his toes.

His eyelids felt heavy. If he closed them, would they ever open again? He hoped not.

He gazed at the image of his mother on his lap. It swam and faded, growing fuzzier as his eyes strained to focus.

Then it disappeared.

AUTHOR'S NOTE

Very few people outside Iceland realize that Britain occupied the country in 1940; I certainly hadn't heard of it until I started writing novels set there.

Royal Marines landed in Reykjavík in May that year and they were soon relieved by the British territorial 49th Division from Yorkshire – nicknamed 'the Polar Bears' – and a Canadian brigade including the exotically named Cameron Highlanders of Ottawa and Les Fusiliers Mont-Royal. At its height, at the end of 1940, there were over 25,000 British and Canadian troops defending the country. This has always seemed odd to me – I would have thought they could more usefully have defended Britain from the Germans just across the Channel. But Major-General Curtis, the commanding officer in Iceland, was adamant they were needed. No one thought to check with the Royal Navy, who were equally certain the Germans could never have transported an invading force to Iceland and, more importantly, supplied it once it had landed.

In the summer of 1941 the Canadians and the British left for Britain, and handed over the defence of Iceland to the Americans. While the Allied soldiers never did anything more than fire at a few Luftwaffe aeroplanes flying overhead, aircraft from Iceland harried German U-boats in the North Atlantic, and Hvalfjördur was the mustering point for many of the Arctic convoys to Russia.

Life in Iceland for the occupiers was tedious – the main enemies were boredom and the weather. But many fell in love with the country, and some fell in love with its people. The same troops landed in Normandy in June 1944 and fought their way through France, so in retrospect their time in Iceland was a period of peace and quiet.

The Icelanders' reaction was mixed. No one likes to be invaded, and many were concerned about the conquest of their women. On the other hand, there was plenty of money to be made, especially once the Americans arrived. The occupying soldiers generally behaved well. Many, if not all, of the population might have agreed with the Icelandic MP Árni Jónasson when he said: 'It was practically a unique example in history of an occupying army which was better liked on the day of its departure than on the day of its arrival.'

Of the books and articles that I read about Iceland during the war, one in particular stands out: *Iceland in World War II* by G. Jökull Gíslason. It is both readable and comprehensive, with short chapters on every aspect of the war in Iceland and interesting photographs. Unfortunately, I believe the book is only available in Iceland. *Wind, Gravel and Ice* by Christina Chowaniec gives an excellent picture of the daily life of the soldiers stationed in Iceland, based as it is on her Canadian grandfather's diary.

The farms of Laxahóll, Selvík and Tóftir are fictional, but Hvalfjördur is very real and, on a good day, very beautiful.

I should like to thank all those who helped me with the research and the writing of this book: Jökull Gíslason, Bragi Thór Valsson, Quentin Bates, Richenda Todd, Liz Hatherell, Lee-Anne Fox, Jennye Seres, Jeff Edwards who drew the map, David Grogan who designed the cover, my agents Oli Munson and Harmony Leung, and, as always, my wife Barbara.

A Message from Michael Ridpath
Get a Free 60-page story

If you would like to try one of my stories about Magnus for free, then sign up to my mailing list. I will send you a free copy of *The Polar Bear Killing*, a 60-page story set in north-east Iceland.

A starving polar bear swims ashore in a remote Icelandic village and is shot by the local policeman. Two days later, the policeman is found dead on a hill above the village. A polar bear justice novella with an Icelandic twist.

To sign up to the mailing list and get your free copy of *The Polar Bear Killing*, go to my website *www.michaelridpath.com* and click on the link for 'Free Download' of The Polar Bear Killing.

For more information on my other Magnus books, please read on...

ALSO BY MICHAEL RIDPATH

Where the Shadows Lie

One thousand years ago: An Icelandic warrior returns from battle, bearing a ring cut from the right hand of his foe.

Seventy years ago: An Oxford professor, working from a secret source, creates the twentieth century's most pervasive legend. The professor's name? John Ronald Reuel Tolkein.

Six hours ago: An expert on Old Iceland literature, Agnar Haraldsson, is murdered.

Everything is connected, but to discover how, Detective Magnus Jonson must venture where the shadows lie...

66° North (Far North in the US)

Iceland 1934: Two boys playing in the lava fields that surround their isolated farmsteads see something they shouldn't have. The consequences will haunt them and their families for generations.

Iceland 2009: The credit crunch bites. The currency has been devalued, savings annihilated, lives ruined. Revolution is in the air, as is the feeling that someone ought to pay the blood price... And in a country with a population of just 300,000 souls, where everyone knows everybody, it isn't hard to draw up a list of those responsible.

And then, one-by-one, to cross them off.

Iceland 2010: As bankers and politicians start to die, at home and abroad, it is up to Magnus Jonson to unravel the web of conspirators before they strike again.

But while Magnus investigates the crimes of the present, the crimes of the past are catching up with him.

Meltwater

Iceland, 2010: A group of internet activists have found evidence of a military atrocity in the Middle East. As they prepare to unleash the damning video to the world's media, to the backdrop of the erupting volcano Eyjafjallajökull, one is brutally murdered.

As Magnus Jonson begins to investigate, the list of suspects grows ever longer. From the Chinese government, Israeli military, Italian politicians, even to American college fraternities, the group has made many enemies. And more are coming to the surface every day...

And with the return of Magnus's brother Ollie to Iceland, the feud that has haunted their family for three generations is about to reignite.

Sea of Stone

Iceland, 2010: Called to investigate a suspected homicide in a remote farmstead, Constable Páll is surprised to find that Sergeant Magnus Jonson is already at the scene. The victim? Magnus's estranged grandfather.

But it quickly becomes apparent that the crime scene has been tampered with, and that Magnus's version of events doesn't add up. Before long, Magnus is arrested for the murder of his grandfather. When it emerges that his younger brother, Ollie, is in Iceland after two decades in America, Páll begins to think that Magnus may not be the only family member in the frame for murder...

The Wanderer

When a young Italian tourist is found brutally murdered at a sacred church in northern Iceland, Magnus Jonson, newly returned to the Reykjavik police force, is called to investigate. At the scene he finds a stunned TV crew, there to film a documentary on the life of the legendary Viking, Gudrid the Wanderer.

Magnus quickly begins to suspect that there may be more links to the murdered woman than anyone in the film crew will acknowledge. As jealousies come to the surface, new tensions replace old friendships, and history begins to rewrite itself, a shocking second murder leads Magnus to question everything he thought he knew.

Death in Dalvik

When sixteen-year-old Dísa is given five bitcoin by her divorced father she is unimpressed: she hasn't heard of the cryptocurrency, and five of anything can't be worth very much. But a year later, when her grandparents are about to lose the farm near the Icelandic village of Dalvík where their family has lived for centuries, quiet, unassuming Dísa is able to rescue it with the profits from her astute trading of her father's gift.

Unknown to Dísa, her mother Helga catches the cryptocurrency bug. Not only does Helga invest in Thomocoin, a new cryptocurrency sweeping Iceland, but she persuades many of her neighbours in Dalvík to invest too, taking a cut for herself.

Helga is found murdered on the hillside above the farm and Inspector Magnus Jonson investigates.

Writing in Ice: A Crime Writer's Guide to Iceland

An account of how Michael Ridpath researched his Magnus detective series set in Iceland: the breathtaking landscape, its vigorous if occasionally odd people, the great heroes and heroines of its sagas, and the elves, trolls and ghosts of its folklore; with a little bit thrown in about how to put together a good detective story.

Entertaining and informative, it's a guide to Iceland for the visitor, and a guide to crime writing for the reader.

REVIEW THIS BOOK

I would be really grateful if you could take a moment to review this book. Reviews, even of only a few words, are really important for the success of a book these days.

Thank you.

Michael